WRONG POISON

A GRACE "THE HIT MOM" MYSTERY

NIKKI KNIGHT

CHARADE
MEDIA

Wrong Poison (A Grace 'The Hit Mom' Mystery), Book 1

ISBN: 979-8-9876847-4-0

Copyright © 2023 by Nikki Knight

Cover by Kent Holloway

ACKNOWLEDGMENTS

I'm honestly surprised and amazed that this book is actually a reality. For that, I can only thank my publisher Kent Holloway and Charade Media (my editors Britin Haller and Halle Smith) for giving Grace a chance, and as always, my agent Eric Myers.

It's been a rough year at my house, with illness and loss, and my family of blood, work, and choice is the only reason this book – and honestly, I – came through. I'm incredibly grateful to every single one of them.

My mother died before this project came together, but Grace was her absolute favorite character of mine. So, this one's for you, Mom.

~ Nikki Knight
2023

CHAPTER 1
IT TAKES A KILLER...

M urder at the Alcott Library Book Sale wasn't a complete shock, as anyone who's ever volunteered for one of these small-town events will tell you.

But it *was* a surprise to see who ended up face-down in the paperbacks...and how she got there.

I'd kind of figured if anyone was going to get killed that day, it would be our perky PTA president when she buzzed over with one flyer too many for the ice cream social, and the bookworms turned on her.

As justified as that would have been, it wasn't the way our nice little fundraiser figuratively collapsed in a heap. Nope. Instead, Obedellia Winch, chair of the town council, collapsed in an actual one in the library parking lot.

It's probably unkind to observe that it was a sizable heap, untroubled by current fashion, so we'll just leave that out and get to the important stuff. Mrs. Winch had been busy upbraiding the librarians, my friends Corinna and Moira, because the only history books were "those touchy-feely *Who Was* things that made everything seem like fun, instead of Serious Important Facts," when she gaped like a largemouth bass and fell over, taking a stack of paperbacks with her.

We may have been short on capital-H History, but we had plenty of romances and mysteries, classic and cozy, including someone's late grandma's collection of Miss Marples, which went with Mrs. Winch.

Moira and Corinna froze.

I didn't.

Maybe it was the recent CPR class or being a few critical feet away. Or maybe it's just the way I'm wired, but I ran right over to help. I always seem to wander in where angels fear to tread.

Until then, it had been a pretty terrific late-September Saturday for the good people of Alcott, Connecticut. We're not the fancy suburb next to Yale, or the one that's become an extension of the campus of the *other* university in New Haven County, Quinnipiac. No, Alcott is a little further up the shoreline, and a lot closer to Old New England, complete with an old-fashioned town green surrounded by lovely historic buildings, including a town hall and the library.

Very pretty anytime, but on a sunny day with the leaves just starting to turn, it looks like a sweet, sleepy place right out of a movie.

And our Alcott Town Council has devoted its considerable energy to keeping it that way, refusing any and all offers of development. Apparently, they're afraid if they allow an Aurora Coffee drive-through next to the drugstore on the strip outside of town, they'll wake up one morning and find a Biggie Mart where the green used to be.

Despite that, and a much larger problem for Corinna and Moira, they're obsessed with keeping taxes down. How obsessed? Well, Mrs. Winch once tried to cancel the entire new book budget because she said if people need recent books, they can go buy them.

Maybe let them eat a little cake, too.

It might have been the simple sight of someone as vibrantly unpleasant as Mrs. Winch silent and still on the pavement that caused Corinna and Moira to freeze.

They're not usually delicate flowers. Corinna, my best mom friend, is the assistant library director and wife of an Army reservist. Not to mention the fact her oldest daughter is thirteen. A woman who has a thirteen-year-old in her home can handle anything.

Moira's no slouch either. She's the library director and veteran of twenty-five years of town budget battles. Plus, she teaches adult literacy classes in the *really* tough part of New Haven most weekends. Her sons are grown and both periodically try to convince her to retire to someplace sunny. No dice so far.

We'd all been pretty happy and excited about today. The book sale is the library's big fall fundraiser, and a major treat for readers in Alcott and even a couple of neighboring small towns. It always draws a big turnout.

Big turnout or not, I would have been there anyway. I'm a lifelong library fan, but since Corinna and I became good friends, I often get drawn in as an extra pair of hands.

Today was pretty much all hands-on deck. Corinna and I brought our kids and put them to work. Thirteen-year-old Imani was handling the YA table, while the six-year-olds, her Cherise and my Daniel, classmates again this year, were stacking kids' books for refills.

Imani was old enough to pretend to be bored out of her mind at some event for the annoying parental unit. Cherise and Daniel were adorably serious, carefully pulling books out of boxes and arranging the piles with impressive precision. Daniel looks like a baby owl with his glasses and tufts of red hair, not that he ever wanted to be considered cute. Cherise, in a bright-pink dress with matching holders on her braids, is well aware she's adorable – and not bothered at all by the fact.

The grownups were busy too. We had a few Friends of the Library volunteers pitching in, and lots of happy book lovers streaming through, stocking up on whatever took their fancy.

It was a definite improvement over my usual Saturday

working on Daniel's latest Lego project with one eye while combing through somebody's sloppy writing with the other. Improvement in style too. I'm enough of a work-at-home mom it was a treat to put on skinny black slacks and a violet waterfall cardigan instead of the leggings (yes, they *are* pants!) and old Penn State Law sweatshirt I wore most of the time.

Even took my black hair out of the ponytail, drew a little liner around my blue-violet eyes, and put on a swipe of fuchsia lip gloss.

I was just a few seconds away from regretting *that*.

"Call 9-1-1!" I yelled, glad I'd just refreshed my infant and child CPR certification to stay current for Daniel.

My shout snapped Moira and Corinna out of their daze. Moira grabbed for her phone, and Corinna joined me on the ground beside Mrs. Winch. Fine by me – Corinna had been my training partner in class the week before.

I'd never had to actually *use* my skills; CPR training was just part of being a decent mom. For sure, nothing like this had ever come up in any of my jobs.

Right now, I run a little copy editing and fact-checking business out of my dining room, but I trained as a lawyer, hence the Penn State Law sweatshirt, and I spent several years as a prosecutor before Daniel was born. I'm even still a member in good standing of the Connecticut bar, although my card does say Grace MacInnes, not my married name, Adair.

Nothing I do is as high profile as my husband's work — he's the defense lawyer you call if you're *really* in trouble in New Haven County — but it's important to me, and I'm good at it.

Apparently, though, neither Corinna nor I is especially good at CPR.

I took the first turn at the breaths, leaving her to compressions without thinking too much about it. We switched positions when we stopped to see if we were having any effect, as we'd just been taught. Nothing.

We took a breath together and started back in.

"I sent someone into the building to get the defibrillator!" Moira's normally dry and cool voice was high and brittle above us.

Corinna and I just kept going, as the siren wail finally began. The firehouse was only a few buildings down the block – the EMTs could have run here. What was taking so long?

Or maybe it wasn't really long at all. Time is weird at moments like this.

"We're here, ladies! Nice work!" I recognized the first medic as the father of another one of Daniel's classmates.

Corinna and I helped each other up.

Her face was tight, a furrow at her normally smooth ebony brow, and her coral lipstick smeared. I bet I didn't look any better, probably worse, since my fishbelly-white skin gets blotchy when I'm upset. And the less said about that lovely fuchsia lip gloss the better.

We shook our heads together.

"Our instructor should be proud of us anyhow," she said, trying for wry and almost making it.

"Damn straight."

"C'mon, Grace." A faint smile played at the corners of her mouth. "Do you *always* have to talk like a Pennsylvania woodchuck?"

"Better to own it." I shrugged.

The high-pitched whine of the defibrillator warming up made us both snap back to the victim.

It was only then I really looked at Mrs. Winch and realized I had a problem. The edge of her eyelids had a distinctive red color. I knew that red line...and knew the only thing that could produce it.

I should. I've killed enough creepy men that way.

CHAPTER 2

DOG IS MY CO-PILOT

T echnically, I am not a hired killer.

I am a consecrated assassin.

Big deal, you still poison people, you say.

Well, yes. And no.

Once a year or so, I remove a vile predator who has managed to escape human justice. Always on a commission from my ancient sisterhood, always under very specific rules, and always without sparking even a hint of suspicion.

The predators must be adult males who've done years, sometimes decades, of damage. And yes, I am paid exceedingly well for my efforts, but no, this isn't really about money.

More on that later.

Never mind my unusual side hustle, I was reminded of my *real* job the minute I got home when Scotchie pinned me to the wall and licked my face.

Scotchie Butterscotch Thor Adair, as he's known on his vet forms, is part golden retriever, part some kind of sheepdog, and part Godzilla. An enormous blond mutt large enough to enforce his will, he watches over us as if we were his herd of misbehaving ruminants.

Fortunately, his will generally involves adoration and the hope of treats. And walkies. Lots of walkies.

We brought Scotchie home from the shelter when Daniel was four because Michael believes boys need dogs. Unfortunately, the boy in question is a little too young to be a real pet parent, and Michael is too busy. Which makes me the home team for Scotchie too.

That day though, he provided an admirable excuse.

I leashed him up, parked Daniel in front of PBS Kids and yelled to Michael that I was taking the dog out.

Michael, who was getting ready for his next big trial, grunted an affirmative. I didn't have to see him to know he didn't even look away from the screen. He knew we were home and not bleeding buckets on his office floor, so everything was fine.

He figured.

Most of the time, Michael's cluelessness is a real asset.

Scotchie pulled hard on the leash, and I had to walk very fast to keep up. Works for me. I think better when I'm moving. I wondered what Madge was going to say.

She and I were going to have to really think fast now. She's my elder, as we call our handlers, passing on commissions and important messages from the Mothers who run the order. After I saw Mrs. Winch's eyes, I texted Madge, and we agreed to meet in the park halfway between our houses. As soon as possible.

I'd never used the code for big trouble. Until now.

Someone was out there using the exact poison we do. The one that no one else is even supposed to know how to make anymore.

All right, so about that consecrated assassin stuff.

My sisters, our little group has never bothered with a formal name because it's easier to keep things quiet that way, have been doing our best to put things right for the last seven hundred years or so. If someone, usually a woman, needs a powerful and deeply unpleasant man removed and is willing to pay our price, it's simple enough. We have a few subtle poisons, still mostly

7

untraceable to modern science, that cause what looks like a natural death.

While we consider ourselves consecrated to the Archangel Gabriel, to the best of my knowledge, no one's ever had any actual contact with Them. Angels don't have gender in the human sense and it's pretty sexist to assume they're male. We're like any other people of faith, we believe in the unseen, we do our best to follow our code, and we support our fellow worshipers.

And no, we are definitely *not* witches.

Over the centuries, we've taken out a half-dozen kings and emperors, a U.S. President or two, and an assortment of dictators, gangsters and captains of industry. Anytime a very bad man seems to just quietly drop dead after apparently evading responsibility for his evil actions, it's probable we were involved.

Henry VIII was one of ours, when wife number six realized she might not survive with her head if she waited for nature to do its work. There was also the corrupt oil company CEO who dropped dead before the trial that would have cost his wife what was left of the estate she'd earned by enduring forty years of beatings. She gave most of it to the poor, with some encouragement from us.

Since I live so close to New York City, I've had a few high-profile commissions myself. The Wall Street creep who spent a couple of decades pinning women to his desk and finally went to trial only to get acquitted? Mine. That TV anchor who had a button to trap interns in his office and walked on a technicality? Him too.

Scotchie saw a squirrel about half a block away from the park and took off. I had to run to keep up, and nearly blew past Madge who was on a bench by the first tree. She looked up from her book and smiled.

"Well, hello." Her sparkly gray eyes swept over me with more than a touch of concern.

If you didn't know that Madge Arsenault was a high-ranking member of an ancient order of assassins, you'd think she was a cute little lady of a certain age, complete with silver hair, LL Bean wardrobe in shades of pink and burgundy, and a sweet smile. She really *is* a semi-retired social worker, and she really is good at her job. The book in her hands was the current hot self-help tome, *Love Yourself and Heal*, which I'm sure she was hate-reading. If Madge wrote the book, it would be *Get Off Your Backside and Heal*.

She closed it. "I'm relieved to see only the dog is wild after that message."

I shook my head. Scotchie had stopped barking at the squirrel and the tree and settled into a stakeout. He'd be busy for a while.

"You may start barking at the tree when I tell you what just happened," I said, sitting down beside her.

"I heard about Mrs. Winch. My neighbor was coming back from the book sale in a tizzy when I left just now." She shrugged. "Sad as it is, it will probably be good news for Moira and Corinna. Whoever takes over as chair can't be as much of a pain as she was."

"It's not the fact she died. It's the way she died."

Madge's eyes narrowed.

"Her eyelids had the red line."

Madge's eyes widened.

"Nothing else produces that," I said, not that I needed to.

"Nothing." She took a breath. "How?"

"That's the big question. We're supposed to be the only ones who know about subtle poisons."

"Revelation from the Archangel." Madge's tone wasn't ironic the way it usually was, a commission or message from the Mothers was usually passed on with that description. And a wry little smile.

No smile this time.

"There isn't anyone else in this area, is there?" I asked.

"No. Eliza MacNeish was the closest. I cleaned out her apartment in the Bronx a couple of years ago."

Madge froze. Stricken.

"What?"

"I put everything in the basement. All the books…"

"Books?"

She took a breath. "Al took some boxes to the library for the sale a week ago…"

Al Kaufman, retired New Haven police officer and general good egg, was Madge's fella (at their age, neither was comfortable with boyfriend-girlfriend) and the first sign of a social life she'd had since she was widowed two years ago. Of course, he had no idea about her other occupation, and it had to stay that way for his safety and hers.

I patted her arm. "Even if it was in the pile, someone would have to be able to read Renaissance Latin to know what it was."

Madge shook her head. "Not this time. Eliza wrote it down in big letters in English on the flyleaf because she couldn't see the recipe anymore. It was supposed to be destroyed."

My jaw dropped.

"If it is not being passed to another sister, the Book is to be burned in the presence of at least one of the Mothers. Preferably more." She put her hands on her face. "Oh, dear Lord. What are we going to do?"

"Worse – what did Moira and Corinna do?"

"You don't think…"

"Mrs. Winch was threatening to cut funding again." I sighed, remembering a few tense words with my friends earlier in the day. "It might have meant one less job."

"I don't think it would have come to Moira firing Corinna." Madge, who was closer to Moira, shook her head. "She'd fire herself first."

"Corinna wouldn't let her." Moira was struggling to keep her mother in a decent facility for dementia, and Corinna and her husband had two jobs in the household. I bit my lip. "But neither of them..."

"None of us knows what anyone is capable of until it happens." Madge held my gaze.

"Well, that's true." A huge golden wave landed in my lap, and a giant tongue slathered my nose.

"Hello, Scotchie." Madge patted his back, and the dog shifted his affections to her.

Scotchie was almost bigger than Madge, but she didn't mind. He adores her, and the scent of her huge orange tomcat Connery is just a bonus. Madge chuckled as the dog licked her face and snuffled at her neck.

If I thought he was a useful distraction, I didn't say so.

After a few moments, she took a breath and pulled back from Scotchie, the concern filling back into her eyes. "All right."

"Not all right at all."

A twist to her mouth. "No kidding. What can we do?"

"Well, we might get lucky and have it ruled natural causes."

"It's been known to happen." She scowled. "I'm not sure I want to rely on luck."

"I'm not sure I do either. We'll still have to figure out who had the poison and make sure they never use it again."

"One way or another."

I wasn't too sure I liked the sound of that, but I nodded. "Yeah."

"Well, then it's a good thing a prosecutor is on the case."

"*Former* prosecutor." I never went back from maternity leave after Daniel was born. Michael and I had both been latchkey kids, and we wanted him to have as much parent time as we could give him. That was supposed to mean a part-time job for me, and Michael pitching in whenever possible from his home office.

It hadn't quite worked out that way.

"But you're still a lawyer."

"Of course." I thought about it. "We can at least make sure there's nothing that points to us."

"Leave no evidence." Madge smiled grimly.

It was one of the big rules – for a very good reason. "Exactly."

"We'll have to do more than that though, with someone out there using our formula."

I took a breath. "They probably don't know it's ours."

"True."

"And who would believe them?" I asked. "Ancient order of lady poisoners, really?"

"Well, there's that."

"All right." I patted the dog's backside, the sign that it was time to get moving. He jumped down. "Looks like Scotchie and I are going to take a quick swing by the library lot."

"Why?"

"It's probably empty or close to it, and it's not a crime scene. I'm going to see if I can find anything pointing to our killer."

"Good idea." Madge nodded.

"I also want to make sure it's just sitting out there, because if anyone starts talking about suspicious death, we'll want to remind them there's no chain of evidence."

"Do you think it'll come to that?"

I sighed. "I sure hope not. But I want to be able to take one of my former colleagues aside and say, look, you can't get that evidence into court."

Madge gave me a sharp glance. "What about witnesses?"

"We're all witnesses to the collapse. That's probably not a problem. I'll have to sniff around to see if anyone saw anything else. I don't want to rattle cages if I don't have to, so let's wait for the M.E."

"Do you know anyone in the medical examiner's office?"

"Not anymore." I shrugged. "But Michael's paralegal does. If it comes to it, I'll ask her."

Madge stood, pulled herself up to her full five-foot height, practically stacking each vertebra into perfect alignment, and setting her face in careful calm. "We can manage this."

"We absolutely can. Do I want to ask what happens if we can't?"

A tiny shake of the head. "Better not to."

CHAPTER 3
AT THE SCENE OF...

T he library was a block further up from the park, an easy enough walk for an energetic dog and reasonably fit human. I checked my watch. It seemed like I'd been out for hours, but the conversation with Madge had taken only ten minutes.

Since I treated Daniel to a nutritionally vile fast-food mini-meal and left him glued to a *Nature Cat* marathon on PBS Kids, I figured I had about twenty more minutes. Longer than that, and there'd be a demand for a snack or attention that would pull Michael away from his case and point out my absence.

Besides, while Michael is mostly oblivious, he is smart enough to know I sometimes use walking the dog as an excuse to take a few minutes to de-stress. For all that he's usually uninterested in my daily mom life, Michael does understand a lot of the weight of the house falls on me and tries to help when he can. He's a good guy.

Most of the problem is he's just too good. These days, Michael Adair is universally acclaimed as the defense lawyer you call when you're *really* in trouble in New Haven County, thanks to a couple of high-profile acquittals of people who were actually innocent – at least of the crimes charged. But that kind of success also requires a lot of work, and someone holding the fort at home.

Guess who.

It's (mostly) okay. I love the guy. Have ever since one Swing on the Green Night in New Haven when this big ginger-haired fella I knew slightly from the law library walked over and asked me to dance. I looked up into those green and gold eyes, and it was all over. He'll even tell you almost the same story, a dozen years later.

Anyway, on this far less romantic afternoon, I had a little room to move. And I needed it.

I needed fudge too. Yes, fudge. I make fudge from scratch late at night sometimes. Okay, usually after a commission. Once the candle is lit, and the appropriate prayers are said for the soul of the subject and the consolation of his victims, I start the sugar and milk in my grandmother's old copper pot.

There's something so relaxing and normal about watching the mixture bubble, tracking the temperature until it reaches the soft-ball stage, then adding the butter and vanilla, letting it cool a bit, and finally stirring – and stirring and *stirring* – until it's smooth, satiny candy. Once it's ready, I have a piece, or two, save out a small plate for the fellas, and freeze the rest.

They have no idea why I do it, but do you know anybody who asks questions when they're offered homemade fudge?

As Scotchie and I zipped up the street to the library, I promised myself I'd thaw a piece from the last batch tonight. Maybe two.

Who am I kidding? I'm making a new batch tonight.

Of course, it's inappropriate to pray that the Archangel would help me hide evidence...but that doesn't mean I didn't do it. Mostly, I was just hoping nobody was at the lot, because it would mean no one considered the site a potential crime scene.

The guilty truly do flee where *no man pursueth*. It's another key point in the assassins' training. *You* know you just made something happen, but no one else does unless you give them a reason – so don't give them a reason.

Mrs. Winch's death was a textbook case.

Considering her age, it was entirely possible her death might spark no suspicion at all. Which would make my life easier, even though it would not relieve me of the obligation to find the person who caused it and make sure they didn't use what they'd learned on someone else. Or share our secrets.

One way or another, I was going to have to catch the killer.

Before it was over, they might wish the cops had found them instead.

I might too.

I really hoped none of my friends were involved.

Right now, though, there was work to do.

The library lot was deserted. The book tables were still in place, and there was no police officer or other authority making sure no one wandered in to tamper with the evidence.

It was entirely possible no one had yet realized there was any evidence to protect.

Up to me to keep it that way.

"Sit, Scotchie."

My giant furry friend doesn't always follow orders, but he will, when he's been moving for a while, lie in a sunny spot and observe for a bit, especially if there's something fascinating like tree leaves moving in the wind. I didn't need long.

While nothing had been moved or put away, someone did have the presence of mind to put tarps over the tables and pull the cash register table into the library lobby. That been the plan for the end of the day because the sale was supposed to extend into tomorrow.

Probably not now.

Probably wouldn't hurt to offer to help with the knock-down tomorrow, now that I thought of it.

First, though, a decent look at the scene. We had a special table for the old books, and I didn't remember seeing anything that looked like it might have been one of ours. But I've heard of people having them re-covered. And who knew what a woman who felt the need to actually write out the poison formula on the flyleaf might do?

There was a full set of the *Book of Knowledge* encyclopedia like my grandparents had, a couple of early 20th century bird guides, and a bunch of 1950's art books from the Met. Several very nice old 19th century classics that might be early or even first editions. What wasn't there, though, was anything resembling the Book.

Might buy the *Book of Knowledge* for Daniel. If I could find a place to put it.

I put the tarp back down and walked over to the place where Mrs. Winch had fallen. The paperback she'd been waving at Moira and Corinna was still on the ground, along with the Agatha Christies, Mrs. Winch's scarf, and a few other bits of debris.

What about that book?

Who Was Abraham Lincoln? seemed harmless enough.

The series was beyond Daniel's reading or interest level right now, but we had a few from relatives who didn't realize that. I liked them; they made historical figures understandable and relatable to kids. Nothing wrong with it.

Well, unless you were Mrs. Winch.

It had landed open, pages down. I bent over, first looking closely at the cover. Nothing to see there. Still, the good bookworm that I am, I picked it up and put it back under the tarp. Can't stand to see a book harmed.

As I turned back, I almost tripped over Mrs. Winch's scarf.

Maybe?

I picked up the scarf, a truly hideous orange-brown ombre crochet that had not matched any of the drab shades of her frumpy outfit – and almost threw it back down. There was a strong scent of some kind of bad men's aftershave. The kind of thing I remembered my grandpa pouring into his hands and splashing on his face after shaving, though his had been light and herbal, more to soothe the skin than scent it.

Not this – this was one of those heavy old-school musky things that makes you think of 1970's singles bars. I read in some magazine ages ago that people, especially men, tend to stick with the scents that remind them of the best times in their lives.

I suppose I'll spend the rest of my life smelling of peanut butter and baby shampoo.

But aftershave wasn't all.

Under the loud musk was something else. Faint and dusty, with a distinctive trace of floral decay. Nothing on earth like it.

Our poison.

It's simple but deadly; we make it from a few common seeds, spices and plants. All you do is apply a small amount to the skin, and it does its work very quickly. The usual procedure is to touch someone's bare arm, or shake hands and slip it onto the wrist...but there's nothing to stop you from putting it on someone's neck.

What I couldn't tell is whether Mrs. Winch was poisoned by the scarf, or if she put it on after she was poisoned. Honestly, I didn't think she would have gotten enough poison from the scarf, but she'd sure gotten a full dose somehow. No matter how it happened, I couldn't leave the ugly thing here. I rolled it up and slipped it into the extra pooper-scooper bag I always carry when I walk Scotchie. It made a bump in my barn jacket pocket, but nothing impossible.

As I moved over to the trash can to take one more quick look for the Book, I couldn't help worrying. My sisters and I are immune to the poison – like some other organic chemicals, you can work up a tolerance with small amounts over time – but an amateur wouldn't know that.

Even if you were smart enough to make it with rubber gloves, how would you get it onto the victim without harming yourself or anyone else? Well, someone obviously did, because the only dead person was Mrs. Winch.

Nothing interesting in the trash can but a red-capped plastic container that might have been the salad dressing from somebody's bag lunch. Except the residue in the bottom was a familiar reddish-brown. Sure, it could have been French dressing, but it might not have been. I scooped it up and slipped it in my other pocket.

Like every mother of a small boy, I always have a couple of wet-wipes on me. Unlike every other mother, I've made sure the brand I use will neutralize any residue of subtle poisons. I gave my hands a good cleaning even as my phone dinged with a text.

I'd have bet my (still-active) law license it was Michael.

It was: Are we out of apple sauce packets?

No. New box on the counter.

Like I said, clueless, but he tries.

I picked up the dog's leash. My secret life would have to wait while I sorted out my daily one.

"C'mon, Scotchie. Let's hit it."

CHAPTER 4
KILLER FAMILY NIGHT

S aturday is Michael's night to cook.

Between his trials, my work at home, Daniel's school events, and everything else involved in running a life, it's tough to manage more than a quick check-in over chicken nuggets during the week.

But on Saturday, he takes over the kitchen, and we have a real family dinner, usually followed by a board game, and later, couple time over wine.

It sounds a little *Leave it to Beaver*, and it probably is.

That's okay; Michael and I both grew up with divorced parents who had to work too hard, and we decided early on we were going to give Daniel as much family time as we could.

Saturday is our night. Period.

When Scotchie and I walked in, the dog's nose perked up, and I smelled trouble.

I should have expected it.

Michael was preparing for arguments in an elaborate corruption trial involving a local developer who paid off officials for a project in Bathport, the next town up the shoreline. Not his usual thing; he was known for near-impossible wins in traditional criminal cases like murders and burglaries. But he loves a challenge, and the corruption case was definitely a stretch.

When Michael's feeling insecure in one area, he likes a win in another.

Which is why the house was filled with the scent of meat, onions, and spices, and (I was sure) the kitchen was a disaster area. Michael had his grandmother's recipe for beef stew with dumplings which takes most of the day, and which he makes only when he's stressed.

It's like my fudge.

"Scotchie! Mom!" Daniel jumped up with a big smile. He looks like a perfect hybrid of Michael and me – his dad's red hair and smile, my blue-violet eyes.

For an instant, I was thrilled with the happy greeting...and then Daniel handed me the remote.

"Dad doesn't know where to find the alphabet songs. He told me to go read a book."

"He's right." I put the remote on top of the TV, just out of Daniel's reach.

He scowled, looking exactly like his dad. "C'mon."

"Read now, and after I talk to your dad, we'll put the songs on."

"Dance too?"

"Have I ever turned down a dance?" I handed him one of the books I'd bought him at the sale, a picture book of cross-sections of all kinds of machines, from drills to airplanes. He took after Michael's engineer father and my machinist grandfather, with an eye for how things work.

"No." He grumbled as he took the book, but as soon as he opened it, his eyes lit up, and he sat down, rapt as I knew he'd be.

Scotchie loped over to his spot by the fireplace, picked up his stuffed duck (a castoff from Daniel) and settled in for a nice relaxing nap.

A crash and a muttered curse from the kitchen told me culinary magic was underway. Or something like that.

I stuck my head around the door. "Everything okay in here?"

"Just fine, Tweety." Michael was holding a big metal bowl, with a few telltale spots of flour on his green sweatshirt.

He looked good enough to eat anyhow.

About six-three and sturdy, but not stocky, with red hair and green-gold eyes, he looks like every romance novel's version of a wild Scotsman. Proudly Scots too – he wore a kilt for our wedding and still puts it on for the occasional Bar Association formal.

He even has a framed Adair clan badge with the family motto *Loyal Unto Death* in his office. We're even more alike than he realizes.

"How go the wars?" I asked.

"There will be dumplings. The texture isn't quite right yet, but there will be dumplings."

There always are. And he's never entirely pleased with the texture. Michael is as driven and committed to perfection in the kitchen as he is everywhere else.

"Good to know."

"You okay?" He put the bowl down and looked at me.

I looked back.

"Got an alert from the *Alcott Advocate* site just now that there was a medical emergency at the book fair."

"Um, yeah. Obedelliah Winch."

"Whoa, not just anyone." His eyes widened. "Town council chair, right?"

"Yep. The one who's been making all the dire threats about budget cuts."

"'If people need new books, they can buy them,'" he quoted in the waspish tone I'd used when I told him about it.

"That's the one. Just keeled over in the paperbacks."

"Ah. Too bad for her family anyhow."

"Yeah."

"C'mere." Michael reached for me.

I let him draw me in, snuggling close and enjoying the reassurance. I needed it, even if not for the reason Michael thought.

It's the alchemy between us. Most of the time, I feel overworked and overlooked, the supporting player in his high-profile life. But every once in a while, he reminds me that he does in fact cherish me. Even if he doesn't show it very often.

"Everything's fine, Tweety-Bird."

I smiled. Only Michael would have come up with that as a nickname for me; I'm tall and dark-haired with sharp features -- nobody's definition of cute. But from that first dance on the New Haven Green, he called me Tweety because of my "big big blue eyes, like the bird."

"Thanks." I burrowed a bit closer, and he rubbed my back. "I needed that."

"Thought maybe."

As I pulled back, I noticed a couple of spots of flour on my good cardigan. Still worth it.

"So, what happens now?" he asked.

"The fair's probably cancelled for tomorrow."

"No surprise there." He nodded. "You can reschedule later... after a respectful interval."

"Exactly."

Our eyes met, and we both smiled wickedly.

"Maybe even do it-" he started.

"As a memorial to her? Yep. I'll suggest it to Moira."

"Oh after what Mrs. Winch put them through, I bet she's already thought about it." He chuckled. "Entirely respectful. And if it happens to save the budget she tried to kill..."

"Exactly."

Michael picked up the bowl and pointed to the living room. "Nice job getting the kid to pick up a book."

"Yeah." I pulled a modest bow. "Corinna tells me the screen-time fights are just beginning. Imani apparently comes home from school, turns on the tablet, and taps away until she grabs it out of her hands."

"What fun." He looked at the dough. Contemplated.

I was dismissed.

"Well, anyhow," I said, trying not to be disappointed the light had just gone out. "I'm going to go do alphabet dances with Daniel."

"Mmm-hmm."

Michael probably didn't even notice me walking away.

In return, I did my best to ignore him a few minutes later when he walked past Daniel and me on his way back to the office while we were conga-ing to "A-E-I-O-U and sometimes Y!"

I can be a little petty too.

By the time the stew was almost ready, I'd literally washed away my irritation with a quick shower and changed into cute house clothes. Amazing what fancy honey-scented bath gel and body cream will do for morale, not to mention a silky purple fleece and the good leggings. I'd bribed Daniel with cartoons until dinner if he cleaned up without complaint, and he was more than happy to take the deal.

My phone rang just as I was slipping my feet into the ballet slippers I wear around the house. Corinna.

"I know you're getting ready for family dinner – we are too," she started.

"Yeah, but I've always got time for you."

"Thanks."

"How are you and the kids?" I asked.

"Kids are fine."

Which meant she wasn't. "But…"

"Horrible thing today."

"Yeah. We're probably going to be processing for a while." I didn't tell her – and I'd never tell her how I knew – but Mrs. Winch's death was now a part of her, and she would eventually grow around it.

"I guess we will. Never thought I'd have to use my CPR."

"Me either."

Shared sigh.

"You know we cancelled tomorrow?" she asked.

"Figured."

"Moira's thinking we just start over in a few weeks."

"Makes sense. We've got the books -- they're mostly sorted and marked."

"Yeah. We'll still have to do the knockdown tomorrow."

And I could use another look at the scene to be sure I didn't miss anything. Not to mention getting a sense of what everyone knew, or thought they knew. "Why don't we all just get over there around noon? After church for us, and after Moira's brunch with her fellas. Brian will probably be free too."

Our other close parent friend was likely trying to decide if he was sorry – or relieved – that he hadn't been there for today's disaster.

"Sounds good. I'll see if Clay can-"

"No, you won't. The Patriots are the early game."

She laughed. "You won't get Michael either – the Jets are too."

"True."

"Which is too bad," she started, her voice sounding tense again.

"Why?"

"Wanted to ask him if he thinks Mr. Winch will sue us. He went after Moira after the ambulance left."

"He did?" I was shocked. Corinna and I had gone inside to wash up and disinfect as best we could (Covid is still out there!) and we hadn't seen the immediate aftermath.

"She told me later. Apparently got in her face and started yelling about suing before he sped off to follow the ambulance."

"Wow."

"That's what I said. Don't you think it's weird he went right there before she was even cold?"

"Sure do. But she was pretty awful, so why wouldn't he be?"

A sigh. "That's true. And she was obsessed with money and spending…"

"So why wouldn't he be? Yep." I took a breath. "Probably just more of the same."

"And people get weird at moments like that."

"True. Might just have been trying to assert some control over the situation."

"Might be as much of a jerk as his wife was too," Corinna said with a chuckle. "Sorry to speak ill of the dead, but…"

"Yup. Hard not to."

"Really hard." She sighed. "So you'll ask Michael what he thinks?"

"Sure. Honestly, Corinna, I don't think he'd have much of a case – the library would be under the town's liability policy."

"I didn't mean to insult you -- I know you're up on the legalities," she offered in an apologetic tone. "But Michael knows the game. He'd know if anyone would take the case, and if there was any chance of it succeeding."

"No insult taken. He's definitely the one to ask about this."

Just then, the attorney in question emerged from the kitchen and waved at me.

I held up a finger.

Michael nodded and twirled a hand in a "wrap it up" gesture.

"I'm sorry," I said, "I have to go."

"Michael's ready to serve it up?"

She knows about his weekly foray into domesticity, just as I know Clay periodically decides to "organize" the pantry. Last time, she couldn't find the applesauce for three days.

"He is," I agreed. "Stew with dumplings."

"I'm going to send Clay to him for training."

"Only if he teaches Michael to do dishes." We've had this conversation before.

26

"Enjoy. I made spice cake yesterday, so we'll at least get a good dessert."

"Okay, you win."

We were sharing a badly-needed laugh when I disconnected.

"Corinna okay?" Michael asked as Daniel wandered over from the living room.

"Tell you later."

"Ah. Grownup talk."

"Unfortunately, not the fun kind."

Michael leaned in and planted a kiss on my cheek, nuzzling in a little. "Hmm…honey bath gel…there *will* be the fun kind."

"Keep a good thought."

He pulled back with the grin that won me all those years ago. "Or a very bad one."

CHAPTER 5
ANGEL IN THE HOUSE

By the time Michael and I finished losing a raucous game of *Sorry!* to Daniel and settled in for that couple-time over wine, neither of us had any interest in, or energy for, serious issues. As we do sometimes, we agreed to leave my book fair mess and his corruption case on the docket for morning and enjoy our few hours together.

Our ability to do that is probably the reason we're still married.

Nonetheless, even though I fell asleep happy and relaxed, I woke up around two with all my concerns flooding back. I've got a good bit more on my conscience than Michael does, after all.

He only *plays* a killer in the courtroom.

Michael was sprawled and snoring. Across the hall, Daniel was in almost exactly the same position, making almost the same noise. Neither stirred when I tiptoed past on my way to the basement.

My treadmill and mats are down there, but that's not why I was going to my little exercise room.

I had more serious business to consider tonight.

Locked in an old footlocker I'd had since college, now draped in a colorful throw and used to hold the candles Michael thinks are "atmosphere" for my yoga practice, are the tools of my true trade.

The Book, bound in gold-stamped purple leather so old it's almost black, looks a lot like an heirloom family Bible, and it is... with a special section added at the back. With it, the necessary equipment: a hot plate and small pot, a mortar and pestle, a couple of empty and clean glass jars, and a few other implements, and that's all. It's enough.

We make the subtle poison for each commission from seeds, fruits, and a few other easily obtainable things. You'd be surprised how many things you touch and eat every day that can kill you in the right combination and concentration. It's simple enough to make when needed, and even if it held its potency (it doesn't), no one wants something like that lying around the house.

We're careful about everything because everything counts.

Hiding in plain sight has always been our stock in trade. From the start, when a kindly nun helped a lady of the manor dispose of an abusive lord, we've been the pillars of the community who are very quietly setting things right. No one suspected the lady because it looked like the lord died of natural causes – and more importantly, because she gave them no reason.

These days, we'd probably call it privilege: people simply won't suspect "nice" – read middle, or upper-middle class – straight white women of most nefarious things without a push. We've always taken that and used it to our advantage.

But the key part of the bargain is you give no reason for suspicion.

That's why what happened at the fair was so terribly dangerous. Our Book, the recipe for the poison, and the whole spiritual grounding of seven hundred years of quietly successful action, had gotten out of the hands of the sisterhood.

I didn't know if that had ever happened before. It couldn't be good for Madge.

Might not be good for me, either.

My eyes traveled to the tiny mark on the inside of my right wrist. If you didn't know better, you'd assume it was some kind of freckle or small birthmark. In fact, it was a brand, a tiny Catherine wheel.

"I will keep the secret until death."

The pledge each of us made when we accepted the brand. It probably sounded better in the original Norman French, but the point was clear.

Just as Madge was called in to oversee the disposal of the Book and other things from the sister in the Bronx, I could be called in to deal with an issue involving her. Only it might not be as simple as boxing up a few things.

I couldn't let myself think about that right now. We had to find the Book.

That was the only option.

Might make some progress on it at the knockdown. I'd be able to take a good look at the merchandise and see where everything had ended up. It could even still be there, though I wasn't fool enough to believe in that kind of insane good luck.

It could well have been sold to someone who didn't know what they had.

That would make getting it back a lot easier.

But if it had gone to some clueless other person, then someone at the library had made the recipe before they sold the Book at the fair. And used it on Mrs. Winch. That left only a couple of possibilities, none of them good.

Or, the Book could also still be in the hands of the actual poisoner. Which might be equally bad.

A whole constellation of things to keep me awake.

Fudge.

This was *definitely* a fudge night.

Upstairs, in the kitchen, the candy-making process did its own magic. Sugar plus milk plus heat is a very specific kind of alchemy, and it's always satisfying to start with a few simple things and end with a delicious treat. The watching and stirring are also incredibly relaxing.

You can't leave it without risking a big messy boil-over, so you have to just stay there and wait. There is no other place to be, no other thing to be doing, than to simply concentrate on that boiling sugar, cocoa, and milk.

When life is pulling you in many different directions, this clarity of mission is extremely helpful. I'm sure there's some fancy psychological explanation for why fudge is my coping mechanism, and honestly, I don't need to know it.

It works.

By the time I added the butter and vanilla, let it cool, beat the candy yet more, and *finally* turned the fudge into the pan I'd prepared with buttered parchment paper, I was feeling much calmer and more focused.

Taking it one step at a time.

Track the Book. Find out if there's any suspicion of Mrs. Winch's death. Make sure there's no usable evidence...and determine who actually used the recipe. Well, and find a way to make sure they kept their mouth shut.

Preferably without the use of subtle poisons.

I reminded myself there are plenty of other weapons out there. Especially in a small town like Alcott, everybody has side deals, scams, and secrets. All I had to do was find out who was involved, and I should be able to figure out how to play them. It's possible to accomplish almost anything with bribery, black-mail, and threats.

Almost.

There had to be a way to protect Madge *and* the sisterhood.

I remembered one of the other key rules of a commission: never give any reason for suspicion. One of my mentors had put it this way: you know you just did something, but no one else does unless you make a slip.

So, don't.

Right now, it was a little too late to come up with anything concrete. I needed a few more hours of sleep and a bit more time to think before I had a plan.

Well, and one more thing.

I put two big pieces of fudge on a plate, for Michael and Daniel, if they woke before I did. And then I took a smaller piece for myself.

Delicious. Maybe a teensy bit grainy, but wonderful as always. Unlike Michael, I'm not given to hyper-critiquing my culinary efforts.

The fudge was great, and everything was going to be fine.

Madge and I could handle this.

We'd better.

CHAPTER 6
IN THE WRECKAGE

S unday started with church. While we consider ourselves consecrated to the Archangel, most of us aren't especially observant. Part of it is the fact we spend a fair amount of time praying privately about our commissions. More importantly, the sisterhood started in a part of Europe that might have been English, French, or something else – and Protestant or Catholic – depending on who was running the place at the time.

Very early on, the sisters came to the conclusion that whatever the prevailing religion was, we would practice it without comment or complaint. It was a really good way to stay off the stake in the Renaissance, and these days, it's just one more way to stay under the radar.

Michael, Daniel, and I go to the Presbyterian church in town, because it's an open-minded mainline congregation. Also, because as people of Scottish descent, we appreciate the historical connection. And Daniel likes the Sunday School.

It's kind of fun to put on a church dress and play upstanding matron for an hour or so. Even more fun when we stop for some kind of treat afterward.

This time of year, it's apple cake at Marla's Bakery.

It was a little too much fun on this particular day though. The after-church chat and the line for cake left me scrambling into my grubby clothes and flying out the door. Not that the guys noticed.

Not even Scotchie. There's something about the Y chromosome and football.

Michael grew up watching the Jets lose with his father, and now he watches them lose with Daniel. Exactly the way he puts it.

Since we do not live under a rock, Michael is well aware of the health and ethical issues professional football poses these days. He's even helped at least one former player through the application process for a settlement – pro bono. But there's something about watching football with his son that he can't quite give up.

Daniel would probably be just as happy with the documentaries on machinery and architecture they watch in the off-season. What matters to him is the dad time.

What mattered to me on that particular Sunday was getting myself over to the library.

At least I was bringing a little good news.

While we were in line for the apple cake, Daniel was distracted by watching one of the bakery girls frost cupcakes, and I took the chance to ask Michael about the possibility of a lawsuit from the newly-made widower Winch.

Michael wasn't impressed, either with the case, or the widower.

"Assuming she died of natural causes, it would be a very long shot legally…and I doubt he's a nice enough guy to sell it."

"I don't think he is." I'd only seen Morton Winch a few times, following his wife into the library and sneering at the new books shelf. Sure, we're heavy on those domestic thrillers that all look alike (you know the cover: some kind of darkened scene with a three-word title floating on it: DANGEROUS DEATH GIRL) but so what? People are reading, and that's what counts.

"Well," Michael said, with the smile that put so many clients at ease, "find something else to worry about."

Not too hard to do that.

As I turned off Main Street and onto the back road that connects the library, the town hall, and several other municipal fixtures, I saw something out of place at the firehouse. Something pink.

For a moment, I wasn't sure what I was seeing.

Then I realized it was a woman. In a pink sweatsuit.

The color slowed me down for a second, but then she shook her straight, expensively blonde, ponytail, and I recognized her. Kryssie Farrar, the princess of the PTA.

I'd thought those velour sweatsuits were OUT, and it sure wasn't the fashion statement I expected from Kryssie, whose favorite colors always seemed to be beige and dark beige.

She blew a kiss back at the building and scuttled to her car, the same huge white *Moby Dick* SUV half the women in town drive. I got a quick glimpse of a short and stocky man as the side door of the firehouse slipped closed.

Even I, who can barely balance a checkbook, could do that math.

Somebody was up to an entirely different kind of no good.

Since I was right at the library turn, I filed the information away for future reference and got my head into the game for my own problems.

I wished all I had to worry about was sneaking around with some hot firefighter.

Not that I would. Clueless as he is, Michael's the only man I want.

Moira's sensible old gray Volvo, and Corinna's Jeep were in the lot already, and I parked my sensible blue sedan beside them. I've never been comfortable driving anything big and certainly don't want noticeable wheels.

Behind me, a boxy, bright-red mini SUV took one of the last few spaces.

NIKKI KNIGHT

About time Brian got on the scene.

"Hey! What on earth happened yesterday?" he called, as I clicked my locks.

"Obedellia Winch collapsed." I shook my head.

"Ugh. No fun." He pulled his Mickey Mouse ball cap more securely over his balding head. Scruffy work jeans and a UConn sweatshirt finished his outfit. "Even for her. Glad I was at work so I didn't have to think about whether I'd do CPR."

"You wouldn't think about it – Corinna and I didn't."

"Probably true. But you're a bit nicer than me."

Not really true. Brian Stein is actually one of the nicest people I know. His daughter is Daniel and Cherise's classmate Zoey, and he's a single gay parent in a town that is, shall we say, not exactly radiant with ally-ship of any kind. But he's always positive, graceful, and just plain fun to be around. A New York ad guy by trade, he inherited a half-share in Loquat's Hardware and moved to town about three years ago, hoping for a simpler and happier life.

It's mostly worked out that way. And he certainly livens up the PTA and Friends of the Library meetings.

(And in case you're wondering why he wasn't watching football, he's a Giants fan, and they were the night game that week.)

"Actually, pal, you're the sweet one," I assured him. "How's Zoey?"

"Off for her Sunday afternoon grandma time. I heard rumors of a Disney movie and nail polish." His blue-gray eyes glowed; he can't talk about Zoey without lighting up.

"Nice. The fellas are watching the Jets."

"Pats at our house," Corinna said, as she stepped out the back door. "And Imani and Cherise actually watch with their dad."

I shook my head. "Whatever."

"Yep. I'm just glad to get out here and get this over with."

"You two okay?" Brian asked.

Corinna and I looked to each other and shared a shrug.

"Yeah," he said. "I know someone who does PTSD counseling if you decide you need it. No shame."

"Not at all," Corinna agreed. I nodded.

"Well, right now, I need work therapy," Moira cut in as she walked over to join us.

"That'll do for me, for sure." I rubbed my hands together.

"Did you get a chance to talk to Michael?" Corinna asked.

"He doesn't think Winch has much of a case – or a chance of convincing a jury. So he suggested we worry about something else."

"Fine by me."

"I'll start moving the closed boxes inside," Brian offered. "Where are we putting them?"

Moira pointed. "That side storage room by the door for now. Hopefully we'll reschedule soon." And fill the hole in the budget, she didn't say.

"I'll start packing up over here," I offered, moving to the old book table, with the idea that if Al had indeed donated the Book, it would have ended up among the vintage encyclopedias and such. I knew it wasn't on the table, but there were two boxes underneath and cause for hope.

"Let's just pack and drag." Moira waved to the mess. "We don't need to be too elegant about it."

Elegant, we weren't.

Madge and I weren't lucky, either.

The boxes under the old book table were just more of the same: old "Classic Library" editions of the dead white men canon, a few fancy cookbooks from some long-ago club, and a few actually very nice art books. But nothing useful.

I dragged the old book boxes into the storage room and moved over to help Moira at the mystery table. It was still a mess, with Agatha Christie, Robert B. Parker, and a slew of colorful cozies all mingling in a dispiriting heap.

"Think it's okay to get rid of this, Grace?" Moira asked.

"I don't know why not." I didn't cross my fingers. "If anyone wanted to document this scene, they would have. You might want to snap a pic or two just to show that the area is flat and safe – just for your own records, but no one can reasonably expect us to keep it as it was."

And I'll happily destroy any remaining chance of keeping the chain of evidence.

"Good point." Moira pulled her phone out of her pocket and took a couple. "Nice having a lawyer around."

She had no idea. I reached for the Agatha Christies. "I'll try to pack these up in some kind of organized fashion."

"Thanks."

Something fell as I scooped the books off the table. I bent down and took a look. A bracelet. A thin white metal chain with a sparkly little pink flower dangle, it looked dainty, girlish.

Not like our Wagnerian victim, for sure.

Nothing I'd seen on Moira or Corinna, either.

"Hey, Moira." I held it up. "Is anybody missing a bracelet?"

"Nobody's asked, but it was pretty crazy. That is awfully pretty. Let's be careful with it."

Moira went in for an envelope.

"What did you find?" Brian asked, breathing a little heavy from dropping off the latest box.

I held up the bracelet.

"Cute. Mom wanted to buy Zoey something like that for her birthday, but I thought she was a bit too young. Might lose it and be all upset."

"Makes sense to me," Corinna agreed. "Imani's grandmother gave her a little gold bangle when she was four, and she lost it. Mourned for months."

"One more reason I'm glad I have a boy," I joked.

"Yes," Brian said with a grin, "but you don't get to play makeup."

"True."

"It all evens out in the end." Corinna's expression suggested she didn't miss boy energy.

"Here." Moira handed me an envelope. "Seal it up, and then let's get done. I want to go home and collapse in a heap for a few hours if I can."

"Your lips to God's ears," Corinna said. "I set the slow-cooker so all I have to do is feed the fans tonight."

"I wish I could collapse," Brian said. "I'm going to get Zoey back on a sugar high with a face full of grandma's makeup."

"And you're thrilled," I reminded him.

"Oh, of course I am." A sigh. "Let's kill this."

If I gave just a tiny wince at his choice of words, I hid it well enough nobody noticed.

CHAPTER 7
SUNDAY NIGHT FOLLIES

If Saturday night is family night, Sunday night finds everyone back in their corners getting ready for the next round. As soon as I returned from the library, the disappointed Jets fans got to work on their respective tasks: Michael holing up in his office with more discovery documents for the corruption case, and Daniel working on an Earth Science project due Monday.

Who are we kidding? It was Daniel and me working on the project which was a poster about his favorite wild animal. The teacher had emphasized the "wild" part because she didn't want a deluge of cat and dog posters.

Daniel had spent the last several weeks gathering fun facts about polar bears and the Arctic Circle, and now, we had to draw and paint a polar bear, then put the facts on a big piece of posterboard. Of course, the sight of paint, colored paper, and all kinds of art supplies got Scotchie all excited, and we came very close to handing in a dog with polar bear facts taped to his coat.

Guaranteed A, if you ask me.

When the dust cleared, and Scotchie was banished to the kitchen with some Fakin' Bacon, we found a great big pawprint on the posterboard.

"Now what, Ma?" Daniel asked, looking like he might just cry.

"Now, we get creative," I assured him. "We'll turn it into a polar bear footprint."

"Wow. Cool!"

I was doing my best with the poster paint when my phone rang. Madge.

"Buddy, I have to take this," I said. "Right back."

I hit the green button. "Hey."

"Hey." Madge's voice was soft and sad. "I couldn't find it."

"I haven't found it yet either. Too early to give up. There are still a lot of places to look and cards to play."

"Any word on Mrs. Winch?"

"Nothing. But nobody asked the library to preserve the scene. That strongly suggests there is no suspicion of foul play."

"How strongly?"

"Pretty strongly." I thought for a moment. "It's very very hard to make a case if the scene hasn't been preserved. A decent lawyer will argue that anyone could have planted the evidence, and a jury will often believe it. There's enough suspicion of the police these days, you know."

"I do. So things are pointing in a good direction?"

"They seem to be. Look, I don't want to give you false hope, but right now, there's every reason to believe this is going to work out all right."

"Really?"

"Really." I put as much encouragement as I could into my voice.

"I wish I shared your optimism," she said. "I'm not even sure when I last saw the Book."

"Well, I know you had some work done and moved everything around last June – maybe it ended up somewhere you didn't expect."

"Could be. I'll take another look in the morning. Al's coming over after he sees the grandkids...and I'm really at my limit right now."

"No wonder," I kept my tone soothing. "Why don't you enjoy some time with him and try to relax. I'll nose around and see what people are saying about Mrs. Winch in the morning."

"Good thought."

"We are going to get through this," I reminded her.

"We have to. I was just starting to really relax and enjoy having Al in my life and now-"

"Now you have a bump in the road."

"Could be a roadblock."

"We don't know what it is," I said firmly. Stiff upper lip. She'd helped me keep mine often enough. Only fair for me to do the same for her now.

I heard footsteps and a laugh. Michael had emerged to admire Daniel's and my work.

"Gotta go. Have a good night with Al, and I'll see you tomorrow."

"Okay. Okay."

"It IS okay."

As I hit END, I turned to see Michael, reading glasses on nose and brief in hand, beaming at his son. I love the watching the two of them together – the big one and the little one, my two redheads. Michael is Daniel's rock star. He wants to be just like dad in every way, so he's proud of his red hair and height instead of feeling awkward or weird, which is wonderful.

He's not always as wild about wearing glasses, but Michael makes a big point of wearing his readers in a deliberate effort to encourage Daniel. So far, it's worked.

"See, Dad, we're making a polar bear print!"

"That looks great." Michael looked to me. "Somebody's getting resourceful."

"Somebody had to. Guess who's been helping us."

"A big blond dog, maybe?"

At the sound of the word 'dog,' Scotchie loped out from the kitchen with a hopeful expression. Daniel and I tensed, both of us moving to protect the poster, but Michael moved to block the dog.

"Here, fella. How about you come watch me work on legal arguments for a while?"

Scotchie recognized the sound of an owner who wanted to pet and pay attention to him – an offer he never refused. Like most of the world, he likes to listen to Michael talk, though unlike most juries, he does it partly out of hope for treats.

Michael and Scotchie trooped off, and Daniel and I returned to placing the fact cards around the polar bear. A few minutes later, my phone buzzed with a text.

Corinna.

Guess who came looking for that bracelet.

Who?

Morton Winch. Said it was his wife's.

I thought about the delicate silver chain and glittery, possibly precious, flower charm and Mrs. Winch's meaty wrist.

No way.

Nope. Weird.

She had no idea how weird.

I hoped nobody else was thinking what we were thinking right then.

"Ma! Tell Scotchie to stop licking the paints!"

I grabbed the blue bottle from the dog, but not soon enough to stop him from getting a nice taste of it. So much for Michael running interference.

Gotta go. Polar Bear.

I win. Lemurs.

You're right.

The paints are non-toxic, so I didn't have to worry about Scotchie's safety. The paint would work itself out harmlessly…if hilariously.

I really hoped that would be my biggest problem for the week.

And yes, I was well aware of what a mess my life must be if I was hoping for blue doggie doo.

CHAPTER 8
DROP 'EM AND RUN

M onday morning brought a return to routine starting with driving Daniel to John Rowland Elementary.

I can't pull up without snickering. The town hasn't been able to agree on a better name, so we're stuck with a school named for a governor who was convicted of corruption– twice. Michael likes to joke they should at least be able to re-name it for someone who was only convicted once.

But in the meantime, here we are at Rowland, which a fair number of parents think was actually named for the Harry Potter author. (Close enough, right?)

If there is anything more middle-class suburban than school drop-off, I don't know what it is. You have to be at least relatively well-off to choose to drive the cherubs to school rather than trusting them to the bus, and inevitably, it turns into a pageant of one-upmanship.

Make that one-up-womanship.

The moms– and they're usually moms– pull up in their giant white SUVs, and dismount in their matching yoga outfits, or neat little dress, or skirt and twinset getups, depending on whether they're "focusing on family," or "picking up a little work." They follow the kids to the portico in small groups, enjoying carefully casual conversations about things that make my brain cells die.

Can you tell I don't fit in?

I'm not an intellectual snob. I'm happy to talk fifty shades of beige French manicure or new Lego sets. Maybe even a little reality TV if it's interesting enough.

But I might as well be from Saturn around these ladies.

I'm taller, older, scruffier, more educated, and oh, yeah, not from around here. It was really ugly until the afternoon Corinna and I found ourselves in the same kindergarten open-house class and clicked immediately.

Now she and I, and sometimes Brian if he has someone to open the store, hang back and watch the show.

This morning, it was just Corinna and me. Brian saw me getting out of the car with Daniel and pulled up alongside, letting Zoey out with a "loveyoubye" to her and a thank-you to me. Not a problem. One of the luxuries of working from home is being able to help out a friend who has a tighter schedule.

Besides, Daniel and Zoey are pals. She's feisty, funny, and kicks his butt at bowling birthday parties. They also both wear glasses, so they're kind of their own little club. Cherise is an honorary member.

Zoey and Daniel ran up to meet Cherise who was a bit closer to the portico with Corinna.

"Another fun morning at the ranch," Corinna's brittle tone suggested anything but fun. "There is nothing like getting a thirteen-year-old girl dressed and out the door."

"Yeah?"

"Oh, yeah." Corinna wasn't going to bring up Morton Winch, and neither would I.

From the small twist at the corner of her mouth, I could tell she was at her limit after another festive start to the day with Imani, and there was no way I'd make that worse. The bracelet would still be there.

"Six outfits before she found one that suited," Corinna continued.

"Okay, you win. I just had to make sure the green striped polo was clean. He'd wear that thing every day if I'd let him."

She chuckled. "You could just buy another one."

"Sold out. Daniel's not the only kid who likes that style."

A clatter of heels behind us.

"Well. What is *wrong* with people?"

Hello, Kryssie.

Normally, we were beneath her notice, since we were by no means the "cool girls" of the PTA. But once in a while she needed something from the library, or someone who might be willing to write a press release, and she sought us out.

Or we were just the first people she saw when she needed to vent about some trivial thing.

Corinna and I pulled our faces into neutral calm and turned.

Yesterday's Pepto-pink sweatsuit was long gone. She was in a beige cashmere twinset paired with a tan plaid skirt, and of course, nude heels. Her hair was neatly banded back, and her no-makeup makeup was perfect, right down to a vaguely mauve "your lips, but better" gloss.

I was back in the Penn State Law sweatshirt and the grubby leggings. I'd been pleased with myself for finding my favorite beeswax lip balm after I brushed my teeth. Honestly, I was pleased with myself for remembering to brush my teeth.

At least Corinna was showing the flag. In comfortable, but dressy, work clothes of a print dress and matching flowy cardigan in warm shades of red, she was elegant as always. Corinna's mother, a teacher like mine, raised her with a very definite idea of how a lady looks and behaves.

So did my mom, but I've slipped a little in the clothing department.

Maybe in a few others.

Anyway, Kryssie was doing her best, as always, to treat everyone as supporting players in her movie, flapping her little hands in a way that emphasized her heavy diamond wedding set and shaking her head.

"Honestly," she huffed.

We waited.

"Can you believe there were no spaces left in the circle, even though it's not even a quarter to eight?"

"Happens." Corinna shrugged.

I pointed to a sixth-grader with an instrument case almost as big as he was. "Band day. Some folks try to get here early."

"Hmph," Kryssie scowled as much as Botox and fillers would permit. Nothing annoyed her more than the idea that lesser humans knew more about what was going on at Rowland than she did. "Well, that trashy minivan is taking up two spaces."

Considering the guy with a Tesla routinely parked between two to protect his finish and Kryssie had never made a peep, I took it for a convenient change of topic.

"It's just a busy time of year," Corinna said. "Ice cream social Friday night, right?"

"Right. And you're both volunteering, of course." Kryssie happily moved on to something she could control.

"Of course," I agreed, being a good girl and NOT exchanging an eye-roll with Corinna.

"Well, look, I need to get Emily and Jaden settled. The agency is working on some big stuff."

Corinna and I managed to fake interested expressions. Kryssie likes to pretend she's a big wheel in local real estate, but in fact, she answers the phones for the Alcott branch office of a much larger agency.

Exactly the sort of cute little job that's expected of her– and I've seen her playing it up as such with women who don't have the kind of professional background Corinna and I do. At least chameleons are honest enough to visibly change color.

"Well, yes. You know the idea for that outlet mall on the outskirts of town is in play again."

I managed to swallow a sigh. The town fathers had been

doing their best to keep any development far from the Green–
but they still wanted all the lovely property tax revenue that
came from retail. It had to be the right kind of retail, though, and
at least as long as Michael and I had lived in Alcott, the town
had been angling to bring in upscale outlets near the interstate,
which had been a great cash cow for several other shoreline
towns.

Those towns had gotten there first, and in Alcott, there
wasn't a lot of unused space for the project. So, the plan always
fell apart over something.

We were about due for another round now that I thought
about it.

I suppose it was better people were talking about that than
Obedellia Winch. Actually, it was very good news. In suburbia,
almost nothing drives the local conversation more than property
values and development.

If people were busy worrying about whether the outlet mall
would be too close to them, or salivating over the potential property tax break, they wouldn't be worrying about an unpleasant
little incident at the book fair. That was good.

Not so good could be the actual loss of Mrs. Winch. She'd
been staunchly and vocally opposed to any kind of development. Having her out of the picture was a major boost for
anyone who wanted to move that outlet mall.

Enough of a boost for them to remove her?

If someone had been looking for a reason to get rid of Mrs.
Winch and got their hands on the Book...

Just about everyone came through the library sooner or later,
after all.

Might be time to take a closer look at the town fathers and
mothers.

And the best way to do that was to head to the hardware
store.

If Brian and Old Man Loquat didn't have some insight, I
didn't know who would.

"Well, can you make sure Emily and Jaden get inside?" Kryssie asked in that wheedling, super-sweet tone she saved for times like this.

"Sure." I sighed. It was no big deal– I was only working on one project right now, and Brian wouldn't be settled in the store for a few minutes. But it was the principle of the thing.

Corinna, who didn't have to be at the library until 8:30, but didn't like giving Kryssie a freebie any more than I did, shot me a little glance. "We'll keep an eye today...we may need a hand another day."

"Oh." Kryssie absorbed that for a second, taking a moment to remember she was part of a community and should act like it. "Well, of course."

We nodded.

"Bye-ees, then!" She fluttered a quick wave at the kids and stalked off.

Once she was out of earshot, Corinna turned to me. "Piece of work, isn't she?"

"Totally. Do you think we're really in for another round on the outlet mall?"

"I know we are." Corinna shook her head. "Clay's been hearing some things."

Clay works at one of the regional banks, so he definitely would hear things.

"Well, here we go." I meant it as a comment on the outlet mall, but just then, the doors opened, and the kids started rushing forward. Every time, it made me think about those deadly crowd crushes you read about, and I was glad to see the teachers wading in to keep some little bit of order.

Cherise blew her mom a kiss. Daniel tossed me a wave. Zoey turned back to us with her shy little smile. And then they were inside.

The day was underway.

And the grownups were free.

"Hi-ho to work we go," Corinna said, turning for her Jeep.

I clicked the locks on the sedan and started it up. Brian was probably opening the store by now and likely had a few minutes of work to get settled. But the day usually starts slow there.

I decided to stop at Louisa's Coffee and get us a couple before swinging over. Actually, three. Old Man Loquat hears and sees everything...and takes well to bribery.

As I threaded my way through the back streets toward the coffee shop, I went past the fire station and noticed a couple of white whales in the parking lot. One looked more familiar than the other. The "My Kid Was Student of the Month at John Rowland Elementary," bumper sticker and one of those goofy family decals in the back window pointed to one person: Kryssie.

Interesting.

And odd. Since the firehouse is so close to the library, we know the guys' schedules, at least a little. I didn't think the same crew would be on this morning as Sunday afternoon.

I don't really care what– or who– Kryssie does on her own time.

None of my business. Lord knows I'm in no position to judge about secret lives.

Still, I couldn't stop a little chuckle. Our perfect PTA princess might just be up to some serious no good.

One more fun fact to file away. You never know when you might need a little information.

CHAPTER 9
HARDWARE AND SOFT POWER

L oquat's Hardware has been on Main Street in Alcott since at least the mid-1800s. And an Old Man Loquat has been in a chair on the front porch, or by the stove, since then too.

The eldest male member of the Loquat clan, usually the retired owner, happily answers to Old Man Loquat and observes everything that happens in the store, and town. The current incumbent, a World War II veteran heading for the century mark, was more than a little suspicious when his sister's grandson inherited a share in the store and decided to get involved.

It could have gone very badly.

Except Old Man Loquat considered he hadn't fought a war to save the world from narrow-minded authoritarians only to become one in his own hardware store. Not to mention, he immediately recognized Brian as a standup guy, which, as Old Man Loquat has been known to say, has nothing to do with who you marry, or don't.

These days, he's Brian's biggest fan, and Zoey's beloved Old Gan.

When I arrived with three large dark roasts from Louisa's, I wasn't surprised to see Old Man Loquat on the porch. It was a little chilly, definitely early autumn in New England, but he's a hardy sort, and perfectly happy in his green plaid flannel and matching fleece vest.

"Gracie!" he exclaimed, his seamed face and still-bright blue eyes lighting up.

He's the only person allowed to call me that. I hate it, but he's earned the rope.

"How are you today, Mr. Loquat?" I asked, handing over a cup. "Brought you and Brian some joe."

He gave the cup a suspicious sniff, part of the ritual. "Smells good. Just plain coffee with a little cream and sugar, right? None of that fancy stuff."

"None."

We shared a grin. Mr. Loquat took considerable pleasure in playing a cranky old man, and no one would dream of denying him.

"As it should be. Thanks, sweetie."

"Glad to. Is Brian inside?"

"Yep. Mixing up more of that pasty beige paint those little housewifeys love so much." He cackled. The fancies and foibles of our local homemakers always amused him. "You'd think once in a while they'd want a nice bright blue, or at least a little yellow. My mother had a yellow kitchen, and it was just lovely."

"You were absolutely right about the yellow trim in my kitchen," I assured him. Even in his late 90s, he still had an eye.

"Just know what looks good." Mr. Loquat raised his coffee cup to me as I turned for the door. "Thanks again, Gracie."

"Always a pleasure."

Inside, Brian was back at the paint station, as advertised, within sight lines of the door, but hard at work.

He looked up with a smile. "Is that Louisa's dark roast?"

"There is other coffee?"

"Not that I acknowledge, for sure." He took the paint off the blender, dabbed a finger of beige on top of the can, and set it aside. Wiping his hands, he stepped out toward me.

I handed over the cup.

"You may just have saved my life. My sanity, at least."

"Here to serve." I took a jokey bow as I opened my own black coffee.

"Thanks for walking Zoey in this morning. I had to get here early and start on the paint orders. People are already thinking about the look they want for their holiday open houses."

"Lord, save us."

"Save me, anyhow. Don't get me wrong, I'm thrilled to have the money coming in, but the aggravation to earnings ratio isn't great with this crowd."

"Still better than the city grind, though, right?" I always worried we'd lose him; he had a lucrative side hustle with web graphics. Sooner or later, I figured, somebody was going to lure him back to New York with stupid money.

"Absolutely. I'm not even a little interested in going back to that." He took a sip of the coffee and sighed. "And nothing is as good as Louisa's coffee."

"Isn't that the truth." Old Man Loquat walked in, carrying his cup. "Still a little chilly out there. And I want to find out what Gracie knows about that mess at the book fair on Saturday."

"She was right in the middle of it, sir," Brian told him. He always addresses his great-uncle as if he were a Victorian patri- arch, just a little sign of respect. "She and Corinna did CPR on poor Mrs. Winch."

"Surprised *you're* still breathing, Gracie." A cackle. "Touching that one could poison anyone."

Too close to the truth there.

"We had to try," I offered neutrally.

"Oh, I know, honey. And you're good kids to give it a shot. But she was a nasty piece of work." He turned to Brian. "Remember how she got her tights in a twist over the blow-up snowmen a couple of winters ago, buddy?"

"Ugh." Brian shook his head. "I'd forgotten about that. Blocking it out from PTSD probably."

"I don't remember this," I admitted.

Brian shrugged, as his mouth tensed. "My first year here. The store had been selling those big yard decorations for a while…"

"People always asked for 'em. I kinda like the things, honestly." A gleam came into Old Man Loquat's eyes. "Our marketing genius here decides to put three of them up in front of the store on Black Friday. Great idea, ask me."

"Me too," I nodded.

"Well, not if you're Mrs. Winch." Brian's tone turned sharp. "Comes marching into the store demanding to know what I think I'm doing to our lovely old New England town."

"Was worse than that," his great-uncle added with a scowl. "Made some crack about what kind of degenerate thinks those things belong on our Main Street. Narrow minded busybody."

"That would be in character," I agreed. "She was all over Corinna when she put up the Pride Month books in the children's section last June."

"Yep." Old Man Loquat's scowl deepened. "One of those. I reminded her that what people do in private is none of her damn business, and we'd darn well display the merchandise any way we saw fit."

"He was pretty great." Brian winked at Old Man Loquat. "She blew out in a huff and came back with a list of the town zoning rules…which do set some height limits, but that's about all."

The elder cackled. "We'd already sold the ten-footer by then."

He and Brian looked like two bad little boys who'd succeeded in raiding the cookie jar.

"So anyway, Gracie, I'm not sure anyone's going to be too sorry to see her gone."

"Especially not some of the folks on the council," Brian added.

"The outlet mall thing?" I asked.

"That was a lot of it," Old Man Loquat said, "but not all."

"Ginny Pescatore has been trying for years to push her out," Brian said. "Same idea as Kryssie from the PTA, only much more so. I think Ginny sees town council as the first stop on the road to the White House."

"Really?" I couldn't hold back a laugh. I only knew Ginny Pescatore slightly; her youngest was at Rowland in Daniel's first year, so our paths hadn't crossed often. She'd always seemed far too busy and important to bother with lesser people like me.

About all I did remember was she had the same very "done" look as Kryssie, leaning more toward peachy tones for her dark hair and eyes...and one actual interaction.

We'd met at my first Parents' Night at Rowland. Michael was talking with a court clerk he knew, and Ginny, who was already on several town boards at that point, asked me what I did. When I explained I'd left the State's Attorney's Office to be at home with Daniel, the light went out.

Like I was no longer worthy of notice.

It was the first, but by no means the last, school function where I was tempted to tell someone about my other job. Or maybe demonstrate.

I didn't have any problem believing Ginny was ambitious. I did have a tough time believing she was delusional enough to think running the town council in a suburban Connecticut town would really lead to a major political career.

But major is in the eye of the beholder. Maybe running Alcott was the White House to her. And if that were true, then she just might be capable of doing a lot of things to make it happen.

"She's annoying," Brian was saying, "but not as bad as a lot of them."

"Better than that crazy lefty guy."

Brian nearly snorted coffee. "Oh, George Germain."

"Yep. That one. Swear he was giving you the eye, even though he's married to a woman." Old Man Loquat was smart enough not to try for a sip.

"Just wanted me to know he's an ally...I think."

"You mean the guy who's always re-posting Bernie Sanders to the parents' social page?"

"Yeah." Brian's mouth twisted. "Everything that's bad about liberal white guys. But he really had it in for Mrs. Winch. For obvious reasons."

"No kidding," I said.

Old Man Loquat let out a creaky little laugh. "Bottom line, Gracie, there's a fair number of folks who probably think the world's a better place without Mrs. Winch in it."

"Sounds like it." And they might be right, too.

"Good thing it was just some kind of medical problem," Brian observed, grinning. "They'd have too many suspects to count if it weren't."

"They'd have to start with the husband," Mr. Loquat, a crime drama fan since *Dragnet*, reminded us. "Wouldn't be the least bit surprised if he was picking up some kind of side action, sorry Gracie."

I nodded, acknowledging the apology for bringing up matters inappropriate to discuss in the presence of "good women." Old Man Loquat's enlightenment only goes so far... and honestly, it's kind of sweet to be treated with a little old-fashioned respect.

"I wouldn't either," Brian said. "I only saw them together once – they were looking at house paint – but I didn't get the sense there was this big loving relationship."

"But after you've been married a while..." I said, wondering if people would say that about Michael and me.

"Oh, I know." Brian's amiable expression faded. He didn't talk much about his husband Jamie who'd died in a stupid pedestrian crash in New York. Too painful. "But it wasn't that comfortable thing you see with longtime couples. You know, where you're still aware of and caring toward each other, but not all crazy in love."

"Exactly," I agreed.

"Brian's right," Mr. Loquat said. "Winch didn't seem to want her around or hear what she had to say. And honestly, who could blame him?"

A yowl from above sounded like agreement.

We all looked up to the shelf over the stove. Jimmy Stewart, the store cat, was awake. There had been a cat named Jimmy Stewart at the hardware store since the 1940's, in much the same way there's always been an Old Man Loquat.

"Jimmy! Come down here, girl," the elder statesman told the cat, who just looked back at him with her big gold eyes.

The current Jimmy is indeed female, a calico cat the fellas found curled up on the porch one very cold morning a year or so ago, not long after the last Jimmy went to the great store in the sky. This cat is far more Bette Davis than Jimmy Stewart: an absolute star and queen of all she surveys. She had less than no interest in climbing down on her own, but when Mr. Loquat reached for her, she graciously consented to be moved.

"Well, I guess I know what my job is for the next little while," Old Man Loquat said as the cat snuggled into his arms and let out a deep happy purr. Even a star enjoys being adored– and knows who really loves her.

"Sure do." Brian gave her a scratch behind the ears and turned to me. "I have to get back to work."

"So do I," I admitted. I leaned in to give Jimmy a pet, too. "Need to get home and buckle down. Got a book proposal waiting for me."

"Good luck." Brian reached for the paint orders. "I've got about a dozen different shades of beige, cream and eggshell today."

"I think I'd rather that," I said. "Trying to clean up this pitch for an historic true crime book."

Old Man Loquat looked up from petting the cat. "Should write your own book, Gracie."

I just laughed that off as I headed for the door. Writing a book was pretty much the absolute last thing I needed to do.

CHAPTER 10
OUT OF THE FRYING PAN

B ack at the house, I walked into an ambush.
Scotchie pinned me to the wall and licked my face with the desperation of a dog who's been deprived of the love of his humans for entire minutes.

I knew, because I'd seen Michael before drop-off, that he'd left a little while before we did to take a good long run with the dog. You might say, what a nice husband, trying to make my life easier by handling pet care, but the truth is the run and Scotchie's adoring company enable him to relax and think. Still, I'll take the help any way I can get it.

Since Michael didn't have to be at the office in New Haven until around nine, and I'd just caught the top of the hour headlines on my favorite New York all-news station, I knew our poor abandoned pup could not have been alone for more than 45 minutes tops.

I also know dog time is entirely different than human time.

While I don't think Scotchie is afraid we won't come back every time we leave, I do suspect our absences seem much longer to him than they do to us. So the enthusiastic greeting made perfect sense.

Once Scotchie decided I was properly re-scented and marked (with a generous coating of blonde hair), he sat down and gave me the big soulful eyes. People tend to think cats are the master manipulators but let me assure you dogs do an excellent job of motivating their humans.

"Of course, you need a treat, sweetheart," I said, walking toward the kitchen and the Fakin' Bacon.

As Scotchie snarfed, I picked up my laptop and started thinking myself into my current project. A true-crime writer from Hamden had asked me to do a fact-check and preliminary edit on her book proposal. It was intended as a new take on a 19th century poisoning case. Unfortunately, the writing was so clunky it was hard to find the new insight, and there were some major inaccuracies obvious to anyone with even a passing knowledge of poison.

Never mind someone with, shall we say, a good grounding in the topic.

But hey, I was getting paid to pull this into something resembling a story.

Not nearly enough for this though.

It's fair to say I wasn't disappointed to hear my phone.

Madge.

"Got a few minutes?" she asked. The brittle worried note was becoming a part of her voice.

I didn't like that even a little.

"Absolutely. Be over there in ten. Mind if I bring Scotchie?"

"Fine by me. Connery won't be thrilled, but he just got his morning Sardine Surprise, so he should just sit by the fireplace and glare.

"That'll work. I don't think Scotchie will get too close."

"Oh, I'm sure he's learned his lesson." She managed a tiny laugh, which was exactly what I intended.

Scotchie, like many friendly dogs, was initially fascinated by Connery, a sizable orange tabby tom named, of course, for Sir

Sean. The first time they met, Scotchie loped over to the sleeping Connery and sniffed at him.

Connery awoke, saw the big puppy nose, and hissed for all he was worth. Scotchie howled, tried to hide under Madge's couch, and nearly knocked it over instead.

That was almost three years ago. Scotchie still never gets within six feet of Connery, and all Connery has to do is make eye contact with Scotchie to get more space.

"C'mon, big guy, let's go see Aunt Madge." I grabbed the leash.

No matter how much Scotchie fears Connery, he loves Madge more.

At Madge's house, the Connery-Scotchie dynamic was the only normal thing.

Connery was by the fireplace, as advertised, dozing and looking almost amiable. Then he heard and smelled Scotchie. He opened his big orange eyes and met Scotchie's eager gaze.

The dog let out a sad little yip and sat down on my feet.

"Poor puppy." Madge smiled, but it didn't reach her eyes.

She was dressed with her usual care, in a lightweight wine-colored sweater and khakis, but she'd skipped the lipstick, and her skin was that greenish color pale people get when they're upset.

Madge motioned me in, and we sat in the chairs near the window, not the fireplace. Scotchie, with his unerring aim for people who need doggie love, walked over to Madge and put his head on her knee, gazing up at her with the unconditional adoration only canines can give.

A snort from the fireplace let us know Connery was aware and not especially impressed. But if he'd been really offended, he was perfectly capable of a more emphatic statement, so we ignored him.

We had much bigger concerns.

"I'm still searching, Grace. Al says he looked through the

boxes before he took them out and didn't see anything that seemed especially important, but…"

"Could it have gotten mixed in with everything you moved around when you redid the office?" I asked. She'd had a home office for her social-work practice for decades, but after her husband died, and her son got a prestigious professorship at Washington State, she did some major renovations, changing an ugly little backdoor to wide glass French doors to the garden.

"Maybe. I moved around a lot of stuff." She took a breath. "I really was kind of a whirlwind. It was my way to move forward."

"So you could have put a box somewhere it didn't belong."

"I could. But I'm also not sure Al would have realized the Book was important."

"Why not?"

"It looks a lot like a family Bible, and he's Jewish."

"Really?" I asked. "Have you seen Brian's family Bible?"

Brian and Zoey were involved in a Reform synagogue in the next town over, Unity, and he'd had a formal naming ceremony for her last summer. It's supposed to happen when a child is born, but Brian and Jamie had been an interfaith marriage and not especially observant. When Brian moved up here, he found a grief group at the synagogue in Unity, and it went from there. During the party at Brian's house after the service, he proudly showed off his family Bible with Zoey's name inscribed below his and Jamie's.

"Oh, hell," Madge said. "In addition to everything else, I'm a bigot."

"Nope," I assured her. "Just a little clueless. We all miss things when we're close to people who are different than we are. Every once in a while, I find myself apologizing to Corinna because I don't understand something that's really important to her."

"Yeah?"

"Yeah. Just part of the deal." I patted her arm. "A reminder that clueless white chicks have to do the work."

Her face relaxed a bit. "Okay, so then we should assume Al would know what a family Bible looks like and would have pointed it out to me?"

"I think so." I sighed. At some level, I was amazed I was having this conversation with the extremely precise Madge. "You really don't remember where you put it?"

"No." She dipped her head, embarrassed. "It was two years ago, a really bad time. I remember packing everything up. I remember seeing the Book on top of a box of other books. Beyond that, all I remember is it was in a safe place. Carl died two days later. I lost a lot."

That explained everything. I took her hand and she squeezed it for a moment. Carl, her husband of thirty years, had been sweeping a dusting of snow off his car when he just collapsed and died in the driveway. He had the usual heart concerns you'd expect for a guy in his 60s– cholesterol a little too high and activity level a little too low– but there was no indication he was in serious trouble until he keeled over.

And yes, I suppose I have to say it really was natural causes and nothing else. We are specifically barred from using our power on family members, and especially husbands– for very good reasons.

Rules or no rules, Madge would never have chosen a world without Carl. They had shared a mutual adoration I admit I envied. Carl was just as absent as Michael, with that big high-powered insurance company job. But he never seemed to take her for granted or ignore her after the first sentence the way Michael did me.

There was just something wonderful in the way he listened to her.

So, it was no surprise she was absolutely crushed when he died. And I had no trouble understanding how she could have lost track of Eliza MacNeish's Book in the middle of all that. But surely it would have turned up during the reno.

"Look," I said, letting go of her hand with an encouraging pat, "you don't know anything until you retrace where you moved everything for the work on the office."

"I suppose."

"And I'll pursue it from the other end. If it ended up at the library, I can find out what happened from there."

I sounded a lot more confident than I felt.

"It's a small town," she said. "Things can't really get very far, can they?"

"Probably not."

"The real problem is somebody used the recipe,"

Trust her to get to the heart of the matter.

"So far, it looks like the authorities are treating it as a natural death."

Madge held my gaze. "It's good that we may not have the cops to worry about, but we still have a very serious problem."

I'd been doing my best not to think about that part, but she was right. "Somebody out there has our poison and isn't afraid to use it."

"Or was desperate enough to try it."

"Not good."

"Not even a little." Scotchie sensed she was upset and rubbed his head against her leg. She scratched behind his ears.

"But who does that?" I asked.

"What do you mean, who does that?"

"Who stumbles on an old recipe and just runs out and tries it?"

Madge stroked the dog's head. Sighed. "The one thing I do remember about all of this is she'd written 'Fast Undetectable Poison' on the flyleaf with the ingredients."

"Of course she did." Such a reckless act would have burned into my brain, too. "Isn't there some kind of procedure for minimizing the damage when a sister falls into dementia?"

"It's never been necessary. Remember, there aren't that many of us, and when someone is in trouble, there's someone available to come in and take care of the few things that need to be handled. Usually, a sister would just take the Book at some point."

"Or the sister would surrender it in case of a very bad illness?"

"Exactly. Eliza MacNeish slipped through the cracks a bit. The Mother who was supervising her died a few months before she did and may have missed how bad things were. Or Eliza may just have been a little sloppy."

I gave Madge a sharp glance then. A little sloppy is forgetting to dispose of a few leftover apple seeds. Writing the recipe and labeling it as 'undetectable poison' is orders of magnitude beyond.

Madge reacted to my look. "Well, exactly. The fact is, she hadn't had an active commission in years – just intel gathering."

I knew that much: Eliza had been the person who sent me the portfolio of information on where to find one of my assignments, a financial scammer with even uglier habits at home. She had kept precise track of his comings and goings, so it was very simple for me to find him at a newsstand and pass the poison with a simple, apparently accidental, touch on the hand.

Elder sisters often do that sort of reconnaissance. There's no one better at surveillance than a little old lady. People never notice them, and they're often great observers.

And besides, nobody really retires from our sisterhood. Some slow down a bit when their children are very young, but once you've crossed the line into our world, you're staying.

It's not like you can leave.

"So, she could have written that recipe on the flyleaf years before," I said. "It does raise a question."

"How anyone would think that's okay. Exactly." Madge shook her head, and Scotchie gave her another warm and soulful gaze. "What a good doggie."

"Everything is better with a good doggie," I reminded her, reaching over to pat him too.

"It's still not great, Grace."

Well, there's an understatement.

CHAPTER 11
KIDS NEED BOOKS

S cotchie and I were home by eleven, plenty of time for me to buckle down and get in a few good hours of hardcore work on that book proposal.

There's something very soothing about polishing prose. Cleaning up the grammar and punctuation, sharpening the descriptions, smoothing out the flow, just generally making it better carries a sort of Zen.

At least for me.

Fact-checking and research is normally just as satisfying. I've spent most of my life doing some kind of research, between majoring in history, studying law, and then working as a prosecutor. It's second nature by now.

Good thing too. My client had missed a few important things and skipped over others that might have helped her. By the time the pickup alarm on my phone went "ding," I was starting to get a handle on it.

But it was going to be a long week fixing this, and not a cheap one for my client.

That was okay; she made a boatload of money with book and movie rights on a lurid divorce and murder case a few years ago, and this historical project was about credibility, not money.

NIKKI KNIGHT

I sent her an email leading with praise for the few things that were working, followed by an explanation of the many things that weren't, and dashed off to the car. Hopefully I'd still have a client when I got home.

But I couldn't lie and let her go out there and make a fool of herself.

Some things I won't do. Actually, a lot of things I won't do.

I know how that sounds, but the fact is, my life, public and secret, works only because I follow very clear rules. If your mission in life is to do things others can't, or won't, you need absolute bright lines, and you must stay within them.

So, I have a code, and I follow it. Even just in small daily things like managing clients.

Anyway, the book proposal could wait. I had a kid to fetch.

Actually two. Corinna was on until 3:30, so I was getting Cherise and Daniel, and taking them over to the library, where they'd amuse themselves in the children's section for the short time until her shift was over. If that gave me a chance to find out what was happening on other fronts, well, that was my business.

While drop-off has returned to almost what it was before Covid, pickup hasn't. I'm sure there's some good reason, but it seems mostly like a way to force parents to sit in the traffic circle for half an hour wasting gas, energy, and patience.

Remind us who's boss.

I always bring a book or check a couple of my favorite news websites while I'm waiting.

One of them is the *New Haven Herald* website. Michael and I are both old-school enough to enjoy picking up the Sunday morning paper on the stoop...but we're also modern enough to know we need to be able to access news in other ways.

And no, neither of us considers anything posted on social media to be news. A side effect of a professional life spent dealing in facts is a deep appreciation for the way those facts are gathered.

I'll admit feeling a little twist of dread in the pit of my stomach when I clicked on the *Herald*.

There hadn't been anything in the Sunday paper, but that's not surprising. Nobody has real local news operations anymore, and anything short of a huge disaster or mass slaughter probably wouldn't show up for a day or so.

So if there was going to be anything, it would probably be today.

Woman Collapses at Book Fair.

Uh-oh.

I quickly skimmed the piece, my gut knotting as I followed the slightly clunky prose. Even a few years ago, newspaper writing was better.

The Alcott Library Book Fair was marred by the collapse, and later death, of Town Council Chairman Obedellia Winch. Mrs. Winch, 60, apparently suffered a medical episode while browsing. Library staff and volunteers rendered assistance, and the Alcott Fire and Rescue Squad rushed her to Yale New Haven Hospital, but to no avail. The second day of the book fair was cancelled and may be rescheduled. Town Council Vice-Chair Ginny Pescatore offered her condolences to Mrs. Winch's family saying, "It's a shocking loss for the town. We're all devastated." An obituary and funeral arrangements are posted in the Remembrances section.

Somehow, I doubted Ginny Pescatore was devastated.

I knew I wasn't.

The fact her death was described as a medical episode, and that funeral arrangements were set was what I needed to hear, at least for now. No questions, and probably no autopsy.

We might not have to worry about the cops.

Reason to hope, anyhow.

"Ma!"

A backpack came sailing through the open passenger-side window.

"Daniel!" Cherise chided him.

I clicked the locks, and Cherise very gracefully and precisely climbed in and scooted over, smoothing her bright-pink floral dress before buckling up, followed by Daniel barreling into his seat. The difference always makes me smile. It's just something in the way boys and girls are wired– even bookish little fellas like mine have this sort of wild undisciplined energy under the surface that girls just don't.

One of the many fun things I've learned as a boy mom.

"How was the day, you two?" I asked.

We chatted about schoolwork and lunches — and what happened when their friend Ella made Braden laugh so hard milk came out his nose —for the five-minute drive to the library.

As soon as we walked in though, I knew things were a little more interesting than I'd have liked.

Ginny Pescatore was at the circulation desk, talking to Moira, and Corinna was in the new books section with a trolley trying to look invisible.

Corinna saw us and quickly walked over to hug Cherise. "How was the day, sweetie?"

"Awesome, Mom." Cherise grinned. "Got a hundred on the math test."

"Nice." Corinna hugged her again. "What I like to hear."

"I got a hundred too, Ma," Daniel said.

"Good job, pal." I hugged him and gave him a big smile, making a mental note to tell Michael and make a little deal of it tonight. Daniel isn't as invested in schoolwork as Cherise, and I'm not sure why. I worry sometimes he doesn't have the same drive to succeed that Michael and I had...but of course, it's pretty silly to have this conversation about a six-year-old.

Let him be a kid, I reminded myself.

Anyway, I didn't have time right now for parental angst.

Moira was giving Corinna and I the desperation look.

"Hey, you two," Corinna beamed at the kids, clearly trying hard to sell a treat. "I just put out a bunch of new books in the kids' room. Why don't you go have a look?"

Sure, it was a bribe, but it was also about as wholesome as

bribes get. And anyone who wants to judge a busy mom for bribery probably hasn't done any parenting.

The kids turned for the door to the Children's Section.

"Quietly," I reminded them, with Corinna adding the librarian glance for reinforcement.

They trooped off.

"What fresh hell is this?" Corinna whispered to me.

"Still the best Shakespearean line ever."

We both collect good lines, not just from the Bard, but everywhere.

"Well, here's Corinna and Grace now," Moira said, the last word coming out almost as a sigh of relief. "Ginny wants to-"

"I just want to thank you for your bravery, both of you."

Ginny seemed all keyed up: brown eyes sparkling, a little natural color fighting with her bronzer, her normally fast speech even a bit more so. She definitely did not look devastated. But the way she was carrying herself like a visiting star sure gave some fuel to Brian's political ambition theory.

"Um, sure?" I offered.

"That's very kind of you," Corinna said. I knew she didn't have any more idea than I did what to say, but she made it sound better.

Ginny gave us this very serious gaze, impressing upon us the importance of the moment, and reached for our hands with hers. "I want you two to come to town council tomorrow night so we can honor you."

I stared.

Corinna's mouth opened a little, but nothing came out.

"It's not just about you two...it's about sending a message. People should be celebrated for helping." A few of the older afternoon readers were looking up and glaring at her. They did not come to the library for celebrating, thank you.

Ginny took a breath and recalibrated, while all three of us cast about for something to say or do. We didn't come up with anything, so Ginny barreled on, apparently oblivious to our shock and discomfort.

"Besides, I really want to make it clear that our council supports the library and other community services. We're not going to have any more of that nonsense about cutting budgets or interfering in how you do your jobs. I may not agree with everything you put out there, but we're not book-banners either."

Moira's face relaxed, suddenly making her look ten years younger.

Corinna's mouth turned up slightly.

I took a breath.

"The praise is very kind," Corinna started in a carefully diplomatic tone, "but not really necessary."

"Well," Moira said. "That is very good news."

Moira's gaze sharpened on Corinna and me. *Do what you have to do to keep this going.*

"It's really very kind of you to want to praise us, and the library," I said, borrowing Corinna's theme. "But why don't we honor the rescue squad too? It's always good to show some appreciation to our first responders."

Ginny looked at me with more than a little surprise. As if it amazed her that I had an intelligent idea. "Why, that would be quite good, wouldn't it? We'll do just that, after a moment of silence in memory of poor Obedellia."

"That's an excellent idea," Moira agreed, recovering her balance. "We really do appreciate the support."

"We certainly do." Corinna backed her boss up verbally, and literally, moving a bit behind Moira. I knew her well enough to know she was actually plotting an escape.

"Well, of course." Ginny crowed. "It's about time we stopped talking about cutting and started talking about supporting."

We mumbled assent, or appreciation, or something starting with A.

Ginny offered handshakes and arm pats all around. "See you all tomorrow night."

As she swept off, leaving a faint trail of one of those incredibly expensive unobtrusive scents, we stood there speechless for a moment.

"New sheriff in town, huh?"

We turned to see Al Kaufman, Madge's fella, walking up with an armful of his favorite Dick Francis books.

That always made me smile because my late grandfather had been a fan too– of both classic mysteries and the ponies.

Al is pretty much the living definition of an adorable older guy, complete with fuzzy gray hair, navy windbreaker, and New Balance sneaks. The only suggestion there might be something else going on here is the New Haven Police Department crest on the windbreaker– and the canny gleam in his brown eyes.

Before his retirement ten years ago, Al had been a decorated detective, known for getting confessions because he made people so comfortable they'd tell him anything. Not exactly the ideal partner for a woman who used to be a hired killer and still supervises one.

Except it's Al.

He and Madge, both widowed, met at the library's Classic Mystery Book Club and bonded over Dorothy Sayers. There were months of cautious coffees and walks in the park before they both admitted what was going on.

It's clear to me, if not Madge, that Al would love her if she felt the need to pick off pedestrians on the town green once a week. Which doesn't mean she'd ever violate her vows – and put both of them in mortal danger – by telling him.

The rules are absolute: we tell no one.

Especially not partners.

Safer that way for everyone.

But Madge, who'd spent most of her adult life married to a loving and clueless guy much like Michael, wasn't really sure how to work a new partner into all of this. So there was a little tension because Al was clearly ready to make a big commitment, and Madge wasn't quite there.

We do live in interesting times. Interesting in the ancient Chinese sense of a curse.

Al grinned at Moira, Corinna, and me. "Nice to see somebody who has a little respect for this place."

"There's that." Moira agreed.

Al gave us a knowing glance. "Take what you can get while you can."

I'd heard a lot worse advice.

Between Ginny Pescatore and this mob scene, there was no way I was going to be able to get another look at the book boxes today. But I might be able to get something from Al if I played it right.

Moira patted Al's arm and walked back to the desk. Back to work.

"How are you two doing?" he asked Corinna and me. "Tough thing for civilians."

We hadn't talked about it, but I knew I was getting pretty tired of being asked versions of that question– and Corinna looked like she felt the same.

"Just fine," she said. "I'm glad we tried."

"Me too. We did what we could." I took a breath. A desperate subject change was just what we needed. "We'll have to finish the book fair some other day."

"Maybe I can get Madge to clean out more of those old books from her basement."

Sometimes it's better to be lucky than good. I encouraged him. "She said you brought over a lot of stuff."

He shrugged. "Yeah. None of it looked like much. Old textbooks. Dusty old encyclopedias– some of those old *Great Novels* club books too."

"I remember seeing the ads for that in my grandpa's *Smithsonian* magazine," I said.

"My grandma had one of those sets," Corinna said, looking

wistful. "They were a thing. Made your house look cultured."

"Exactly," Al agreed. "Figured somebody else could benefit from them."

"That's the whole point of the book sale." Yes, I will be the next Captain Obvious.

"And somebody looks everything over to make sure nothing valuable gets mixed in, right?" Al asked.

Corinna took that one. "Moira did when she was setting up. A couple of years ago, we found a first-edition art book."

"Wow," I said. I hadn't heard about this.

"Yeah, the owner said they'd donated it, and it was ours. So, we sold it, paid for the fancy new book shelves, and of course, the plaque."

"Nice," Al said.

"Yeah." Corinna smiled. "I know Moira's found a few family Bibles over the years too. She looks them over, finds the name, and sends them back to the families."

"Should save heirlooms, even if nobody really wants them right now," Al finished with a definite nod.

"That's it. My older sister ended up with Grandma's family Bible," Corinna said. "She wanted it. Somebody always does."

"Well," I added, "it's important. Family stuff."

"Exactly." Corinna looked back at Moira. "I need to go wrap things up for the day. See you later, Al."

"See you." He shot her a mini-wave, then turned to me. "Got a sec, Grace?"

"For you, a full minute." I really like Al. Just as Madge has been gradually letting him into her life, I've been slowly adopting him too. My father and grandfather died before I was a teenager, and my uncle is in California living with one of my cousins these days, so I could use some elder statesman influence in my life.

He grinned briefly, but then his face turned serious. "I'm thinking it might be time to give Madge a ring."

"That's wonderful!" Anywhere but the library, I would have

let out a cheer and hugged him. As it was, I contented myself with a pat on his arm.

"Well, I'm still not sure she's going to say yes…"

"She'd be nuts not to," I assured him. Just please don't ask until we resolve this hot mess, I thought. Madge could be so upset over the missing Book she'd screw up this wonderful new start. Yikes.

"Well, I'd like to think so," he said. "Problem is, I'm not sure what kind of ring she'd like. I know what you get if you're twenty-five…but what do grownups do?"

"Hmm. Could you give me a little time to look? I'll go online and find you some ideas if you want."

Buy us some time to settle things so you two can get your happy ending.

Al's eyes widened with interest. "Sounds good to me. I was thinking something more like one of those nice eternity bands, they're pretty, and you don't feel like you're hauling a big rock around every day."

He nodded to my left hand where I wore a channel-set diamond band with my wedding ring. Michael was still clerking when we got engaged, and he bought me a Scottish Luckenbooth ring– crowned twin hearts that look a bit like a claddagh — instead of a diamond. The channel-set was a tenth-anniversary gift, pretty, practical– and because it was very good diamonds in platinum, every bit as valuable as the average big rock.

"Good idea." I ran a finger over my ring. "There are a lot of nice things out there. I'll email you some pics."

"Sounds good." He met my gaze very seriously. "On the Q.T., okay? I want it to be a surprise."

"Of course. I'm very good at keeping secrets." You have no idea how good, my friend.

"Good to know." He squeezed my hand. "Thanks. Have a good afternoon."

"Better now."

CHAPTER 12
THE MOTHER OF ALL PROBLEMS

Unfortunately, things got noticeably worse later that afternoon.

My phone buzzed with a text from an unfamiliar number about half an hour after Daniel and I got home.

Calling you in five minutes. Make time to talk. Message from the Archangel.

It was not, of course, the actual Archangel.

It was something much more serious.

I made sure Daniel's milk glass was full, put out an extra cookie because pre-emptive bribery was the best way to buy a little time and went into the kitchen to wait.

Four minutes and forty-five seconds later, the call came.

"Hello?"

"Grace, dear." Even in her nineties, Professor (now Emerita) Sally Munroe had a huge, creamy voice that just embraced you. In the lecture hall or courtroom, it had been amazing, especially in combination with her huge, clear, light-green eyes.

I'd been thrilled when she took notice of me in class, praising my work and legal reasoning. And when she asked me if I might be interested in pursuing justice in a more direct way, I was honored to be the one she chose.

"Professor Munroe." It would be unthinkable to address her any other way. "Always good to hear your voice."

Some of the other Mothers, the elder women who run our little order, prefer to be called Mother, but Professor Munroe earned her title the hard way, and she'll take it to the grave. Not unusual. Of the half-dozen Mothers on the Council, four prefer Professor– or Judge.

We know of the Council's existence, but sisters usually only have direct contact with the Mother who chose them. (That's the preferred description– recruited carries some unpleasant subtext, and Professor Munroe once explained that "chosen" is the exact translation from Norman French.)

Under normal circumstances, I would not have been surprised to hear from Professor Munroe. The Feast of the Archangels is on September 29th, and it's traditional for the Mothers and sisters to exchange small gifts. Madge and I always give each other funny cat cards and candy.

Professor Munroe and I have a more reserved relationship. I send her an elegant and expensive arrangement of her favorite yellow roses, and she sends me a small succulent– the one plant even I can't kill. Since Michael has a close friendship with one of his mentors from Yale Law, he doesn't see anything odd in my annual exchange with Professor Munroe. And he likes the succulent garden in the kitchen window.

"Always good to hear your voice, as well, Grace. Though I would prefer it under more pleasant circumstances."

"This is not an advance greeting for the Feast of the Archangel, is it?"

"No. I'm sure you're aware Margaret has an issue."

Madge, much respected mentor and handler, becomes misbehaving Margaret to Professor Munroe. Not a good sign.

"We may have a situation," I admitted. Lying was not just wrong, but infinitely more dangerous if detected. But that didn't mean I had to put the worst spin on things...or give away anything the Mothers didn't already know.

"That's a way to put it. If there is truly a copy of the Book out there…"

No need to complete that sentence. Interesting though, she had not mentioned the murder. We might have some room to move.

"We're doing all we can right now, Professor," I assured her. "It's not entirely clear the Book is indeed missing."

"Margaret told me she is searching her house again, and you are searching the library. We will assume for the moment it is all nothing but a misunderstanding of some kind."

"Thank you."

"Of course. I have great faith in both of you. You've done wonderful work. I have no doubt you'll put this right."

No need to state the implied threat.

Better not to, in fact.

"We will, Professor."

"Just what I wanted to hear. Of course, you'll accomplish this as quietly as we do all things, and with no unnecessary action."

Action, in this case, meant poisoning. She wasn't going to flatly tell me not to kill anyone I didn't have to, though that was clearly what she meant. "I understand."

"Excellent. I would suggest as soon as possible." She took a breath. Considered. "If I do not get good news by the Feast Day, I will have to tell the other Mothers about it…and there may be a need for some corrective measures."

"I understand."

"I'm not worried, Grace." Her tone was confident, with only the tiniest edge of menace. "It's you and Madge. Failure is not an option."

"Not at all." Not even close. We said our goodbyes and ended the call.

After that little donnybrook, I was glad Michael was staying late at work. I needed some time to calm down and work through the anxiety from this. While Daniel read one of his new books, I decided to take a yoga break before getting back into the editing.

Something had to help.

It did.

Mostly.

As I stretched up into crescent pose, the sleeve of my sweatshirt slipped back revealing the brand, and reminding me, if I needed a reminder, I was carrying seven hundred years of secrets.

We receive the brand when we join the sisterhood. My ceremony was a small gathering by the fireplace at Professor Munroe's house, and probably much like any other induction. You don't survive seven hundred years in secret by making a big deal of things.

Professor Munroe, two other Mothers, and the retired sister who would be my first handler were the only people present, arriving at 5pm like an ordinary ladies' tea. Which, honestly, it was.

Well, except for the branding and vows.

Even that was very simple.

A small prayer to the Archangel, and then Professor Munroe turned to me, holding what I'd have taken for a slim silver pen if not for the glowing red tip.

"Do you willingly accept the brand and join the sisters in their work?"

"I do." I held out my right wrist. None of that sinister left nonsense with this crowd.

"Then join us now and make your declaration."

She took my wrist, turned it over, and raised the iron.

"I will keep the secret unto death."

Everybody flinches a little and thinks it's going to be terrible.

It's not. A quick jab, a sizzle, and it's over.

Then smiles all around, hugs, and handshakes.

Finishing, of course, with tea and cake, like the nice ladies we are.

And a few days with a bandage and healing ointment, there's no point training assassins only to lose them to a nasty infection. It was a real concern in the days before antibiotics.

You're probably wondering about the Catherine wheel I mentioned before. It's in memory of the one sister who broke the rules.

Her name was Elisabeth, and she did it all wrong for the right, the best possible reason: her child.

This was back in the time of Henry V, early 1400s, in the neighborhood where we got started, which was owned by England after Henry and his archers pulled off the underdog win at Agincourt.

It was Henry's troops, and specifically, one of his commanders who drove Elisabeth to it. Like most of the women in the early history of the order, she was a "goodwife," the spouse of a man with some property and position in their community. I don't know much else about her, except she was younger than I am now and had several kids, including a fourteen-year-old daughter.

In our world, that's a girl. In theirs, a woman. And even if she weren't a woman, things happen when the king's army comes through, all charged up with victory and testosterone.

We know that. And we're not supposed to go off freelance when terrible things happen to our families. But after Elisabeth's daughter was attacked by Henry's commander, she wasn't thinking about her vows, or her calling, or her sisters. She was thinking about her daughter and her own vengeance, not the Archangel's.

What's the point of having power if you can't use it to make things right for the people you love most? I have no trouble understanding why she did it, and neither do the rest of us.

The commander might well have met the criteria for a commission anyway. But Elisabeth didn't talk to her elder or her sisters. She just made her way to his camp and his tent, walking in sweet and modest, a village goodwife with a humble request, and slapped him across the face.

That, of course, was enough. He obligingly dropped dead. His men thought witchcraft, because they would. They didn't have enough wood for a stake to burn her, but with the machinery of war, they were able to improvise a wheel.

The story goes they kept asking her if she belonged to a coven and if there were other witches. They even offered to let her live if she gave them the names of women who were conspiring against the king. She knew they didn't mean it, and she gave them nothing. Not a word. The only thing she said was two syllables at the very end. Her daughter's name.

Catherine.

Soon enough, the other sisters in the neighborhood found out what had happened. And though they knew Elisabeth was wrong for what she did, they owed their safety to her brave refusal to give them up, so they branded a tiny wheel on their wrists in her memory and passed on the story.

As we still do.

They also promised each other if a sister's family suffered some grave insult, they would take it to the Mothers, and another sister would be permitted to avenge her in the fullness of time, when it was safe and appropriate to do so. It has happened often enough over the centuries starting with the commander's liege lord. If you've read the play, or seen the movie, (Olivier or Kenneth Branagh, both far hotter than the real king!) you've learned Henry V died of dysentery. With some help from us, thanks.

All that leaves one simple and unmistakable lesson: no matter what, and no matter who is involved, you must use the power only as you have promised in your vows. You must trust that God, the Archangel, or your sisters will eventually give justice.

It's a heavy lift, but no heavier than the power we've accepted, after all.

And if, God forbid, you find yourself on a wheel one day, you remember Elisabeth and you give them nothing. Nothing.

"Mom! That boring news show is on!"

Daniel's voice brought me back to the 21st century.

Scotchie came over and nudged me out of warrior pose, and I almost fell on my face.

"C'mon, Mom! Make it go away!"

Since the *PBS NewsHour* lead was politics, I couldn't agree more. I picked up the remote and switched to a show with robots and the alphabet.

Much better to stay safe with the consonants for a while.

CHAPTER 13
DEEP IN THE NIGHT

I f there's one thing that makes marriage worthwhile, it's the conversations in the wee hours. I'm not downplaying the importance of having one person in the world who's promised before God and these witnesses to be on your side, no matter what. And I'm certainly not brushing off the sex.

But for my money, the main reason to get and stay married is the talks that happen in a moonlit room after a whispered: "You awake?"

Michael, who'd been monosyllabic with exhaustion by the time he got home that evening, was the one who woke me around two. I'd been having some nasty little stress dream, and he might have thought he was doing me a favor by waking me.

He was.

"Hey." I slid over to him and burrowed into his arms, enjoying one of the other major marital privileges. Until I met Michael, I'd never been involved with a really big guy, and it was a treat for me after a lifetime of being as tall or taller than my date. Even now, a dozen years in, I loved feeling surrounded and protected.

Yes, that's probably sexist and retro. And no, I have no intention of raising my consciousness on this one. I take my fringe benefits where I can get them.

"Hey." Michael pulled me in a little closer. "Sorry I wasn't very talky earlier."

"You managed to ask Daniel about his day and read him a story at bedtime, so you hit your marks."

"Dad marks. Not so great in the husband department."

"It's okay. I'm a grownup. I know you're busy."

And I usually like it that way.

"All right." He nuzzled my hair. "Just don't want my Tweety-Bird feeling neglected."

Only he could make the silly nickname sound hot.

"Doing just fine." I assured him. "This corruption case is really taking over everything, isn't it?"

"It's a little bit of a stretch, you know. I usually do straight criminal. Murder, robbery, drugs. This one is anything but straightforward. And the Feds are involved even though it's state charges...so I have to nail down everything."

"I'm sure you're doing fine."

"It's just a lot." He took a deep breath. "These things are tough to prove, so I know they wouldn't go ahead without a tight case. Which means I have to find little holes. Pull on a loose thread and hope it falls apart. And it all revolves around financial crap and real estate."

"Not your favorite."

A bitter laugh. "If I wanted to do real estate and financial law, I could have gone into that. I wanted to be out on the high wire."

"Fighting the good fight."

"Something like that." He shook his head. "Nobody likes criminal lawyers until they need one, you know."

"Not quite true. I think most people understand you're doing an important job."

"Tweety, you're a little too nice sometimes."

Not all the time. "Well, anybody who's ever actually met you knows you're a standup guy."

"There's that. This one is just a bear. They're trying to drown us in discovery in hopes we'll give up and plead to the top count just to make it go away. So, Annie and I are up to our eyeballs."

"Do you need another pair of legal eyes?" I asked. While I often helped him with opening and closing arguments, whether editing or just as a sounding board, I didn't usually do anything else. Michael, his paralegal, and his two part-time clerks were all he needed most of the time. He was extremely proud of his solo practice, and with good cause.

"Well...aren't you doing that book proposal?"

"Yes, but I can always find time for you."

"Let's see what happens in the next load of discovery. I may just take you up on it."

"Good. Be a nice change from editing and fact-checking."

"Are you bored, Tweety?"

Not right now, in the middle of the mess with the Book. But on any given day in my little mommy world? Boredom wasn't even the right term. Ennui? Desperation, maybe. "Sometimes."

"Would you like to pitch in once in a while?"

I wasn't sure if I did...and I was even less sure he wanted me to. "I could, but only if you're really sure you want me."

Honesty, what a concept.

He turned a bit so I could see his face, his eyes dark and bottomless in the moonlight filtering through the blinds. "I always trust your judgment. That's never a question."

"Okay..."

"But you're carrying the home-front. And running your little– your editing operation. It's a lot too."

I caught the 'little.' I also caught him correcting himself and being careful– and appreciated the effort.

"It *is* a lot," I said. "But I also like the idea of using that legal degree of mine."

I watched his face. Curious. Careful.

"So maybe I invoke your expertise when I can. Like the discovery on this corruption thing. It's all-hands."

"Sounds good."

"I like it. Do I have to pay you?"

"Hmm." I smiled as he drew me to him. "For now, you'll just owe me."

"Or I could provide some in-kind services…"

CHAPTER 14
JUST ANOTHER MOM DAY

No surprise, it was an extra-caffeine morning.

It seemed like the alarm went off five minutes after I fell asleep in Michael's arms, and I just couldn't clear the fog from my brain. I forced myself to walk twenty hard minutes on the treadmill, to no avail. My first cup of black coffee was gone before Daniel even woke up, and it had zero effect.

My second cup was breakfast while Daniel polished off his morning waffle and sausages– thank heaven for the freezer and microwave.

Michael wandered into the kitchen while I was loading the dishwasher.

"Hey, Tweety."

"Morning."

"*Good* morning," he said with a grin.

The Y chromosome is an amazing thing.

I lose sleep for couple-time and wake up feeling like I got hit by a truck.

He loses the same sleep for the same reason and wakes up like a ray of sunshine.

If I ever use my secret skills on him, it'll be because of a morning like this.

"Yeah." I poured more coffee into my cup. "Want some?"

"Save me a cup for after I run. He leaned close and whispered in my ear: "Don't need anything else to charge me up right now."

I managed a smile as he walked toward the door. I do love the mope, after all.

"Hey, Tweety, can you head over to the town offices after drop-off?" he asked as he took Scotchie's leash from its hook.

"Why?"

"It's the forms we have to send in for the re-assessment. I finally got them filled out, so you just need to swing by the office."

Swing by the town office, which doesn't open until nine on the dot, stand in line, and then find the appropriate functionary. Oh, sure, I've got time for this in the middle of everything else.

Anything I might have said at that point would have been exceedingly unkind.

Instead, I bit my lip and finished loading the dishwasher, then moved into getting Daniel ready for the day.

I probably said two words to Michael before we left, just a quick "love you" on the way out the door.

No matter what, that never changes. And I never hold that back.

I know too much.

"You look like I feel," Corinna said as I walked up to the portico.

"That good, huh?"

"Yep." She did have just a tiny bit of puff under her eyes. "I didn't sleep too well either, with this ridiculous town council thing coming up tonight."

"Yeah, there's that." I couldn't stop a small shudder. "And a little too much late-night conversation."

"If someone could explain to me why the guys wake up all cheerful, and we wake up tired, I'd appreciate it," she said.

"You too?"

"Oh, yeah."

"I think it's the Y chromosome," I observed.

"Makes sense to me." A sigh. "Hate getting old. Remember when we could stay up all night and work all day?"

"Not since college."

Just then, Zoey bounded past on her way to Cherise and Daniel, followed by Brian.

"Hail the conquering heroines," he said.

"Oh, not you." Corinna glared at him.

"Really?" I glared too.

"Ginny Pescatore was in yesterday afternoon. Told me I should come out tonight to support you two at the big woo-hoo."

"You're not-" Corinna started.

"Can't close early in the middle of leaf season, sorry." His eyes twinkled. "Unless you need me there for a little moral support."

"We'll survive," I assured him. "Unless your idea of moral support involves liquor."

"Hard liquor," Corinna added. "We're going to need it with Ginny."

"Oh, you are. Should have heard her yesterday. She's having a really hard time hiding how happy she is about taking over."

"I didn't think she was hiding it at all," I said.

"She's muttered a few appropriate words about poor Mrs. Winch now and again," Brian said. "Something like it was just too bad to be taking office under these sad circumstances."

"Uh-huh." Corinna shook her head.

"This is going to be a nightmare." I rubbed my forehead, which was beginning to throb. I wondered how much aspirin I could take before I risked liver damage.

"Just remember," Brian said, "it's not about you. It's her show. Just stand there and smile a little, and before you know it, it'll be over."

"Close your eyes and think of England?" Corinna asked.

Shared head shakes on that one.

"Well, don't you all look happy today!" Kryssie clattered up, today in a little beige shift dress topped by a cream-colored cardigan. Emily and Jaden scampered off, probably glad to get away and mix with people who weren't nearly as perfect as their mom.

"Positivity is the key to everything." Corinna delivered the pronouncement with a grace I could never have managed.

"Oh, yes. Is that Maya Angelou?" asked Kryssie.

Corinna cut her eyes to me, and Brian winced a little.

"Nope," Corinna said, "just a general observation."

"Oh. Well, anyway, it's a good thought. I'm practicing positivity now too. So important to meet the world with openness and grace, don't you think?"

We nodded.

Not much else you can do with that.

"It's going to be very exciting around here soon, you know," Kryssie assured us. "The outlet mall is probably going to be a go this time."

I'd believe that when I saw it.

The stampede for the door began just then, saving us all from further unpleasantness.

With a little more grumbling, Corinna, Brian, and I went our separate ways.

I checked my phone as I reached the car. A new text from Madge:

Got a minute to swing by?

As it happened, I had 59 of them, since someone with More Important Things To Do had stuck me with the assessment forms.

Be right there.

I had just enough time on the drive to Madge's to find one of my favorite 90's songs on the radio and relax into the chorus before I parked.

One of the many problems with suburban mom life: you can

spend your entire day in and out of the car and never really get a second to yourself.

Of course, that wasn't the real issue here. But it was better to think about the small stuff right now.

Connery yowled at me as Madge let me in, clearly disappointed he wasn't going to get to bully Scotchie today.

An unhappy cat was the least of our problems.

"I'm sure it's not here," Madge said, folding onto the couch. "It's out there and somebody used our recipe to kill an innocent woman."

"Not that innocent," I reminded her.

Madge gave me a very serious glare. "By our standards, which are the only ones that matter here, she was innocent."

"True enough." I took a breath. "Okay. The good news here is nobody thinks the death was anything other than natural."

"Well, there is that."

"The item in the paper yesterday suggested funeral arrangements are set– calling hours Thursday and private service Friday -- which means probably no autopsy."

"So we may be in the clear with the cops."

"We may just be."

"We're still going to have to find out who did it," Madge said. "And deal with them in some way."

"Is there a specified way?"

"I don't think there's a rule for any of this." She clenched her fists, unclenched, and rubbed her hands against her legs. "I'm not sure I want to find out."

"Will the Mothers care how we settle it as long as we settle it?"

"I don't think so. If we can assure Professor Munroe the Book has been found and destroyed and no one is planning to use the secrets in it, we'll be fine."

I nodded. Good. We still had a way out of this. If Moira or Corinna had done it, I could find a way to keep them quiet without resorting to something more serious.

I sure hoped so. It's one thing to remove a vile predator. It's another entirely to turn those skills on a friend.

"All right," Madge said. "So, the Book has to be at the library."

"Or somebody bought it." I thought for a moment. "I didn't see it in the piles we picked up Sunday, but that doesn't mean much. I'll get another look in the storage room as soon as I can. Probably tomorrow."

"Okay."

"And at this point, I have no problem telling Moira something valuable got mixed in with the donations. I'll say it was a family piece of yours."

"Sounds good." She nodded. "Do you think Moira or Corinna…"

"I really hope not."

"But if not them, who?"

"If the Book was in the fair boxes, it could have been a lot of people. Ginny Pescatore volunteers at the library, Kryssie Farrar is around a lot– even Mr. Winch collects pulp paperbacks, so he might have had access."

Madge's face brightened a little. "Good money is on the husband?"

She's been around retired cop Al too long.

"The spouse is always a good possibility. Even if we can't figure out how it happened." I shrugged. "But actually, I think better money is on Ginny."

"Really? People don't usually kill over politics."

I just looked at her.

"Well, they didn't use to anyhow."

"And it's not politics. It's ego and power, which is everything in a small town."

"Maybe money, too," Madge said. "Isn't the outlet mall thing in play again?"

"I've been hearing that."

"All right." She sat up a little straighter. "So we have some ideas."

"We sure do." I took a breath. "I have to go to town hall anyway this morning. Maybe I can pick up something."

"Sounds good."

Her phone made a twinkly noise.

"Al." Despite everything, she smiled. "We're going for a walk in the park."

"Nice."

The smile faded. "Maybe not so nice."

"Why, for heaven's sake?"

"I think he wants to marry me, and I'm not at all sure about that."

"Really?" I asked. "Don't you think that's where you've been going all along?"

"I suppose. I've counseled any number of people about starting over after loss…but now it's me, and I just don't know."

I met her gaze. "Do you think it's because of everything going on right now?"

"Maybe."

"So don't make any decisions until we settle this. And enjoy the good stuff."

She looked at me for a moment. "That is almost exactly what I would tell a client in this situation."

"See how good you are? We will get through this." I patted her arm.

"Failure is not an option."

Madge's tone echoed Professor Munroe's words too.

We both knew if we didn't resolve this, we probably wouldn't have to worry about resolving anything ever again.

I didn't know how it would happen.

It would look natural or accidental.

But it would almost certainly happen.

Not something either of us needed to dwell upon right now.

"Okay, then." I managed a light tone. "We've got stuff to do.

At least you get to go for a walk with your fella. I have to go to town hall."

"Better you than me." She had the same stiff-upper-lip smile as I did.

Outside, it was one of those perfect New England fall days. Clear blue skies, sun filtering through trees just starting to turn. The kind of day where it's almost impossible to believe anything bad could happen.

We all know how that works.

My phone tweeted as I got in the car. Of course, that's Michael's ring.

"Tweety, I think there's something wrong with Scotchie."

I sat down in the car, not turning it on, my stomach tightening. "What?"

"When I took him for a walk just now, well, it was blue."

"What was blue?"

"Um, you know. The poo."

A man who had spent three full years as the backup diaper changer, including any number of poorly timed explosions, could have been expected to handle this a bit better. But he'd clearly gotten enough distance from the gross stuff that he'd lost the vocabulary a bit.

I laughed. Not just at his discomfort, but with relief.

"What's funny about blue poo?" He sounded a bit hurt.

"What's not funny about blue poo?" I asked. "Remember, he ate the poster paint?"

Michael let out a sigh. "That's all?"

"Absolutely all. It's non-toxic. Just kind of disconcerting."

"Oh, yeah."

If I thought blue poo was just-deserts for this stupid town hall errand he'd saddled me with, I kept my thoughts to myself.

CHAPTER 15
GET IN LINE

M adge's house is a few blocks back from Main Street, and a few turns from the back street that winds behind the fire department and library, and ultimately to town hall. I'm not telling you this so you can make a map of Alcott. I'm telling you this because of what I saw when I passed the firehouse.

A familiar giant white SUV, and Kryssie. And a firefighter.

A great big firefighter.

Not the guy I'd seen Sunday.

I didn't think it was anyone I knew, but I wasn't a hundred percent sure.

The "who" may have been open to question, but the "what" wasn't.

It looked like something out of one of those trashy movies that used to air late at night on cable. Not that I'd ever watched them, of course.

Wow.

I was honestly amazed at the brazenness. Not to mention the logistics. While I'd seen it on TV (with my college girlfriends, okay?) I hadn't thought actual real-life people did that.

Impressive.

And risky. Probably part of the fun, though.

This time of day, most of town is busy at work or school, and this end of the road is very quiet; it's a residential area, and people coming to town hall usually turn in from the other end of the street.

But it was still pretty adventuresome of Kryssie and her friend to be out there in the parking lot. Clearly, adventure was part of the fun.

Well, then.

None of my damned business, I reminded myself.

Not that I minded the distraction. Or the delicious gossip.

As I turned into town hall, I couldn't help giggling. Our perfect PTA princess had some very nasty habits indeed.

Not to mention much better balance than I had.

Like many New England towns, Alcott started out with a gorgeous 19th century town hall and added to it in the middle of the next century. In most communities, the additions are carefully thought out and harmonize as much as possible with the original building.

Not Alcott.

The addition is an impressively ugly blond brick box with an oddly-angled glass atrium thing joining it to the back of the old one. There's a reception desk that always seems to be empty (budget cuts!) and signs pointing to the row of municipal offices crouching across the back of the gorgeous old building housing the council chamber and the town manager's office.

It's a depressing beige corridor most locals only visit when they have some kind of important errand, like registering to vote, or completing a mortgage re-fi…or turning in forms for the property tax re-assessment.

All of the offices look alike, and the signage isn't great, so I inevitably get lost.

If you suggest I block the layout from my memory because I'm mad at Michael for leaving this mess to me, I'm not going to argue. There's sure something going on.

This time, I was at least after nine so I was able to walk right in, which is not possible even at 8:59, because our town functionaries are very precise. Or something.

I remembered the tax office as being the first one on the left, so I stepped in there and right into a line of other people who had the same idea.

There is no time when you're waiting in line.

I always find myself thinking of that old episode of a scary TV show where everybody thought they were in the waiting room for hell...only to find out it actually WAS hell. Pleasant line of thought, especially right now.

"Excuse me!" an officious little voice called.

I turned and saw a small woman with a lot of well-highlighted blonde hair, gazing at me with more annoyance than curiosity. "What are you waiting for?"

"Just to hand in the re-assessment forms," I said with a friendly smile. I always try to be as nice as possible at times like this. A lot of folks are surly to town officials, and kindness usually eases the path.

"Well, you're in the wrong place. This is the zoning office."

Not with this one. Her tone was pained.

"Sorry."

"Never mind." She sighed dramatically. "We're the first office in the row. It happens all the time. Next one down on the right."

She pointed and something on her wrist caught the light.

Not just anything.

A bracelet that was either the one I'd found in the library lot, or its exact twin. The one Morton Winch had picked up later.

Well, then.

"Thanks," I said, keeping my voice friendly and steady. "Sorry to make your day tougher. I know you folks work hard here."

"We're up to our eyeballs here in zoning. You have no idea."

"Probably not with everything going on in town."

"No kidding." She sighed. The conversation was over.

But I'd gotten plenty.

"Thanks – really."

She'd already dismissed me, which was fine. I headed down to the correct office, dropped off the forms, and started back into the atrium.

Interesting.

Maybe interesting. The bracelet was pretty, but it wasn't an uncommon style. Those little chains with elegant sparkly things hanging off them are big right now. It was always possible I was trying to focus on Morton Winch because I didn't want it to be Moira or Corinna.

Both of whom still had the best opportunity to get that Book. And more, to make and apply the poison.

"Grace!" Ginny Pescatore was descending on me, marching down the hall from the old part of the building, wearing a beige blazer and carrying a couple of folders. The Important Woman in action.

"Hi, Ginny."

She looked me over. Today it was a purple hoodie that dated back to my pregnancy with newer space-dye leggings that picked up the color. Comfortable, and not at all inappropriate for a stay-at-home mom day. But more than enough to get me a sneer.

"You're going to change for tonight, right?" she asked. "You–"

"I was an assistant state's attorney. I think I know how to dress for a town council meeting," I reminded her.

An uncomfortable twitch. She didn't like being reminded that I was a real person, not just somebody's cute little mom.

"Well, fine. I'm sure it's a big moment for you and Corinna. It's a big moment for me, too– we want to do this right."

"You want to do this right," I echoed. Interesting she was seeing this as her big moment as much as (or more than?) Corinna's and mine.

"Well, yes. It's important to set the tone."

"Important to remember Mrs. Winch also."

The full two seconds of blank stare told me everything I needed to know about Ginny Pescatore. "Oh, of course. We need to keep her in mind."

"Right, then." I nodded to her. "I've got a lot of work to do this morning. One of my clients has a deadline for a proposal coming up."

"I don't want to keep you." She patted my arm and gave me what I'm sure she thought was a sincere smile. "Have a good day. We'll see you tonight."

"Yes. Thank you."

Well, that was one productive stop.

I took the way home past the firehouse. The white SUV and the show were of course gone. That was something too.

I'm not an astrology person. I think I'm a Scorpio, but because my birthday is November 22nd, I might be a Sagittarius. Anyhow, despite my skepticism, I do think there's something to the whole idea that the world aligns in weird ways every once in a while and strange things happen.

This morning had sure been a good illustration of that.

Things did not get materially better when I got home.

They did get bluer though.

A woof from the dining room greeted me when I arrived, and Scotchie loped to the door, clearly hoping for a walk. Which he would have gotten immediately if his mouth hadn't been bright blue.

For a second, I was terrified.

"What did you do, Scotchie?" I asked.

He licked my hand and left a light slick of blue. Enough that I recognized the smell.

Poster paint. I ran into Daniel's room, and sure enough, Scotchie had managed to nudge the paint jar onto the floor and get a taste.

Only the blue one.

"What's with you and blue paint, big guy?" I asked,

surveying the disaster. As Scotchie messes go, it was relatively minor. But still.

.I made very serious eye contact with Scotchie.

"NO. Not for you."

He let out a little whimper and hung his head.

"I just don't want you to get sick, fella." I scratched his head. "C'mon. I'll get you some Fakin' Bacon while I clean up."

Scotchie rubbed his head against my leg, leaving a nice blue smudge on the leggings. Well, they– and I– are washable.

As I grabbed some orange cleaner and paper towels, I sighed. We were in for more blue poo.

Probably no better than I deserved, honestly.

CHAPTER 16
LADIES, TAKE A BOW

A fter that little run-in with Ginny at town hall, I was
seriously tempted to show up at the council meeting in
my Penn State Law sweatshirt. But I figured I should at least try
to look like a grownup, so I got out the purple suede jacket and
black pants I wear for parents' nights. I didn't know when
Michael would be home with all the discovery-dumping, so I
started water for pasta and chased Daniel into an early shower,
figuring I'd have to bring him along.

Then, a surprise.

"When were you going to tell me?" Michael asked by way of
greeting when he walked in just before six, arms behind his
back. "Or were you going to let me read it in the *Herald*?"

"I-" I wasn't sure where to go with this.

"The council secretary called the office to make sure I would
be there tonight. You didn't think I'd want to be there to applaud
my wife?"

"No, but you're in the middle of discovery and-"

"And you're my wife, Tweety. And I'm proud of you. And
there's no way Daniel and I won't be sitting there cheering you
on tonight. Here."

He was holding out a bouquet. Big pink roses like the ones

I'd carried at our wedding.

"Oh." I thought I might just burst into tears right there. I took the flowers. "Thank you."

"I know I miss a lot, Tweety, but you don't really think I'd want to miss this, do you?"

"I didn't really think about it, Michael. I thought you were busy and…"

"C'mere." He pulled me close, careful not to crush the flowers. "I miss a lot, but that doesn't mean I don't love and support you. And I want to be there tonight when you get some attention for a change."

"Okay."

"Okay." He leaned in for a kiss.

It was probably supposed to be a quick, everything's okay kind of kiss, but it's us, and the guy had just given me roses for the first time since Daniel was born, so I'm not going to apologize for the fact it was a good bit more than that.

If I hadn't heard the pasta hissing like it was about to boil over, something else might just have.

"Okay. To be continued later," I said, snapping back into mom-on-duty mode.

Michael grinned. "Definitely."

An hour later, we were in the council chamber, sitting two rows back from the front with Corinna and her family on one side, and Moira on the other, getting a very good civics lesson. If you want to know why people aren't doing their part in their towns anymore, just go to a local board meeting.

Ginny Pescatore, in the glow of her battlefield promotion, was trying to run everything as if it were her own little movie. Unfortunately, several other members of the council were in their own, entirely different films. One appeared to be a horror flick from one of the right-wing news channels: Burl Brewer, a cranky middle-aged white guy with a beard, wanted the council to pass a resolution condemning drag queens, apparently out of some concern we were about to be invaded by RuPaul.

Don't I wish.

From the other side of the table, Gerald Germain was fighting the bearded dude and pushing for his own resolution to condemn Columbus Day. In majority-Italian New Haven County, Connecticut, that wasn't going to get very far, no matter how much folks get– and support– the idea of honoring Indigenous people.

I'm not sure how long they spent re-fighting the culture wars. Long enough that all of us interested guests started staring at the agenda we'd grabbed on the way in, to see when we might finally get to take our bows and leave.

One of the items after our recognitions caught my eye:

Discussion of Outlet Mall Proposal with Brixton Ventures.

I elbowed Michael. "Brixton? As in Todd Brixton?"

"His company." Michael squirmed, and no wonder. Todd Brixton was the defendant in his corruption case. The last thing Brixton, or the guy defending him, needed was to have him pop-up in a current project. Especially not tonight, when Michael was very deliberately playing the part of supportive husband and trying not to call attention to himself. "Todd didn't tell me they were actively pursuing this again."

"No?"

"No." A scowl that meant there was going to be an uncomfortable client conference soon. "I would have advised him to wait until the case was resolved."

"So would I."

"Anyhow," Michael said, "that comes up after you guys. We'll be home by then, and I don't have to deal with my client until morning. Leave that mess to me."

It might have sounded patronizing, but this time, it wasn't. He was relying on my understanding as a fellow lawyer to know he could not say much about what his client was up to. In his own weird way, Michael was showing me some professional respect.

"All right, people!" Ginny Pescatore snapped, pounding her

gavel. "This has gone on long enough. We can return to Columbus Day and drag queens at the end of the agenda. It's not right to keep our brave first responders and helpful good Samaritans waiting all night."

Columbus Day and the Drag Queens would be a good name for a band.

Probably not what I was supposed to be thinking right then.

Burl Brewer and Gerald Germain traded one more insult, ('Commie' and 'Bigot' if you're keeping score,) and shut up. For now.

Ginny ignored them and turned a radiant smile on the audience, and not incidentally the camera from the New Haven TV station. I hadn't noticed it until now. Pretty much the last thing I wanted to see.

Corinna gave me a wide-eyed glance that was probably exactly the same expression as I had at the moment. Starting to feel like a deer in the headlights.

"Now, we'd like Mrs. Hill and Mrs. Adair, as well as our fine gentlemen from the fire department to come up here."

There was something in the way Ginny said "fine gentlemen" that made me take a good look at the firefighters as I walked to the front of the room with Corinna. It looked like most of the department was here, not just the two guys who'd worked on Mrs. Winch, all in uniform and all looking quite spiffy.

Suburban-mom fantasy objects for sure.

And at least one suburban-mom's real hobby.

Kryssie wasn't present. Probably working on the ice cream social…or bringing perkiness to the poor. Too bad. I would have enjoyed seeing her reaction to the lineup.

"Of course, we appreciate the amazing, life-saving work our first responders do every single day," Ginny continued. "Let's have a round of applause for them."

The room erupted in appropriate acclaim, Corinna and I exchanged glances and started clapping too.

"And, we'd like to give special recognition to fire and rescue squad members Phil Brando and Kyle McHendrie."

The other firefighters gave them a shove to the front of the line and started applauding.

The big guy I'd seen with Kryssie the other day was one of the ones in the back. As he applauded, I saw a ring on his left hand. So Kryssie wasn't the only one breaking her vows.

Understand, I don't get to judge people. And it's none of my business what kind of deals couples make in a marriage. But I do notice things, and it might be important later to know that Kryssie was helping herself to somebody else's husband.

If only because the wife might have something to say about it.

"C'mon." Corinna grabbed my arm. "We go together, or not at all."

"Um, yeah."

"And now, we'd like to offer praise and congratulations to Assistant Library Director Corinna Hill and library volunteer Grace Adair, who selflessly jumped in to give CPR to Mrs. Winch and did all they could to help her."

With the applause and eyes focused on us, Corinna and I managed modest nods.

"They're truly the very best of our town."

We're something, all right.

Ginny marched over to us and handed us certificates, no doubt printed out in the town council office earlier today, and shook our hands.

Please don't ask me to say anything, I thought. Corinna had the same expression of abject terror. We both said a quick, graceful thank-you, and did our best not to back away.

"It's okay," Ginny said. "I'm not expecting you to speak."

Oh, thank God.

"Appreciate it," I replied.

"Well, it wouldn't be fair, would it?" Ginny asked in the dismissive tone she used for me.

"Could be interesting, though," Corinna said. She'd caught it. "You know Grace was with the State's Attorney's Office before she decided to take a stall to raise Daniel."

"How family-minded of you," Ginny said. "You must miss it."

"Some days I do." Some days I'd rather be practicing my other profession. I took a breath. "It was very satisfying to get bad people off the streets."

"I'm sure it was. And now you're...home."

She said it in the same tone someone else would say "medieval dungeon." It wasn't worth pointing out she was home too, in between her local political efforts. Her work was Important.

I have to put up with that attitude from Michael once in a while because I'm married to him. I don't have to put up with it from Ginny.

"Anyway," I said, "it's very nice of you to honor Corinna and me. We were just doing the right thing."

"Exactly," Corinna cut her eyes to me so subtly Ginny didn't notice. "It's no more than anyone should do."

"And everyone should," Ginny pronounced. "So honoring you will encourage the next person."

Encourage them to run screaming in the other direction if it involved something like this.

Ginny turned to the firefighters then, her eyes lighting up with a flirtatious glow. "And you fellas. So wonderful to have you working for our town..."

"Nice job, ladies." The fire chief and his lieutenant came up to us and shook hands. As we made polite conversation, I realized the lieutenant might have been the guy who was with Kryssie on Sunday morning. And he had a wedding ring too.

It was starting to feel a little like a soap-opera in here.

"Well done." Moira appeared behind us, holding two nice bouquets of small sunflowers. "From the friends of the library."

"Aw, thank you," I said. This was the most flowers I'd had

in...forever.

"These are gorgeous," Corinna turned the bouquet side to side for a good look. "I love these."

"So do I," I agreed.

"You deserve it." Moira leaned closer. "If only for putting on a smiley face and dealing with Ginny." I looked to Corinna. She was thinking the same thing: it would take a lot more than sunflowers.

"Thank you all!" Ginny called. "Another round of applause, please?"

Then it was time to leave. Corinna and I and our families worked our way out of the room, all very relieved to leave the development– and culture– battles to our elected officials.

Moira had to stay because the library budget was on the agenda, but the rest of us were more than relieved to make it out to the stairs and get some of the cool evening air.

Michael and Clay, with help from the kids, spent a few minutes commiserating about the Jets' latest disastrous loss, while Corinna and I processed a little.

"Glad that's over," she said.

"No kidding," I held up my bouquet. "The flowers are nice though."

"Clay got me roses, too."

"So did Michael. He said the town council secretary called him at work to make sure he was here."

"Clay got the same thing." Clay, as a bank V.P., keeps just as long hours as Michael, if for different reasons. "Apparently they really really wanted the big moment."

"Ginny wanted her thing."

"Exactly. Always nice to be a prop."

We shook our heads together.

"All's well that ends," she said. "We're taking the kids for ice cream...want to join us?"

"Great idea. They might as well get something out of it."

"So should we."

CHAPTER 17
WE'RE UNDER HERE SOMEWHERE

The next morning was one of *those*.

Every busy mom gets them sometimes: the kind of morning where everything breaks in exactly the wrong direction as you're trying to get the kid fed and packed, the spouse out the door, and your own act together.

Daniel didn't *want* oatmeal, or French toast sticks, or a waffle for breakfast. I finally settled him down with leftover spaghetti and meatballs, which meant I had to come up with a new plan for his lunch.

Fortunately, he's not in a nut-free classroom this year, so I could just slap together a peanut butter sandwich and send that.

In the middle of all of this, Michael appeared asking if I could zap his breakfast burrito for the road. I could zap something for sure.

Then Scotchie discovered if he got up on his hind legs, he could eat the heads off my roses from last night.

As I chased him away, my phone pinged. New ideas from my client who had no concept of time...or just assumed I was at her beck and call because she was paying me.

It was all enough to make a mom lie down in traffic. If she had time.

I wasn't the only one who was having a day either.

At drop-off, Corinna was well into her description of Imani's crying jag because her favorite sweater was in the hamper when Brian pulled up.

"Can you two make sure Zoey gets in? I've got to get my great-uncle to the urgent care."

"Of course." We weren't trying for unison, but it happened that way.

"What's wrong?" I asked.

"Jimmy Stewart clawed him two days ago, and it's not healing properly. Probably no big deal, but with someone that age..."

Corinna and I nodded.

"And you have to make him go," she said. "My dad was the same way."

"Yep." Brian sighed. "I wanted him to go at the end of the day yesterday, but he wouldn't. So I told him we'd go this morning. No arguments."

"Did he buy in?" I asked.

"He will."

We had no doubt as he sped down the traffic circle.

"I'd almost think we were paying for our big moment last night," Corinna said.

"Did you enjoy it?"

"Other than the ice cream afterward, no."

"Uh-huh. So why would we be punished?"

"Good point. Pretty interesting to see the town council at work, though."

"No kidding. Amazing anything gets done around here."

"Amazing they didn't kill each other." She shook her head. "If Mrs. Winch hadn't dropped dead from natural causes..."

I looked at her. There was nothing unusual in her tone. Nothing to suggest she was doing anything other than enjoying an edgy joke. And maybe she was. Or maybe she was misdirecting. Two can play that. "But she did, so we don't have to worry about anyone hauling the rest of the council off to jail."

"Good point. Lord knows what the next batch would be."

"It's hard to imagine worse, but…"

"Yeah."

"Yeah."

The bell went off, and the stampede began.

"And we're into the day," I said.

"See you after pickup," Corinna started to go, then turned back. "Thanks for getting Cherise."

"Not a problem at all."

"And thanks for sorting today. I think Moira's got a little bit of a bug about restoring order."

I shrugged. "Could be worse things."

"True."

"Might want to change your shoes by then, though…or at least one of them." She grinned and pointed to my feet.

I had on one black ballet flat and one silver.

I'd just grabbed shoes out of the hanging organizer in my closet, assuming if they were in the same spot, they were the same shoes. Oh, well.

We were both laughing as I ran to the car, only now noticing that my walk was just the teensiest bit lopsided.

Coffee, I promised myself. A nice big cup before I start work on the proposal.

Once I was back in the car, my phone tweeted.

"What's up?"

"They just dumped another tranche of documents on us. Can you take some?"

"Sure." Nice to be asked, but did it have to be right now? I guess it did.

"Good. Annie will email the first batch to you."

"I'll let you know what I've got tonight."

On the drive home, I planned out my day. With my client firing off ideas, I could just send her a quick acknowledgement, then skim through the proposal and mark places that needed work while the documents downloaded. That would make it a lot easier when I got back to it later.

As it turned out, I had plenty of time to do the markup, because there was an incredible amount of documents associated with the case. Annie was kind enough to start with the main information on the case and a full document list, then flag what she was sending to me.

It was still an awful lot.

It's a well-known strategy for prosecutors and some civil lawyers: drown the opposition in paper. Michael's opponents in the corruption case appeared to be raising it to high art.

After I took a quick read through the charging affidavit and got a basic sense of the case, it was clear the prosecutors wanted this to be a records case. That is, a case where the proof is clearly visible in records the defendants have filed and sworn to be true.

No surprise. As any number of white-collar crime prosecutors can tell you, they're easy to prove, and usually end in a quick plea because it's tough to convince a jury that documents don't mean what they say they do.

Especially since they usually do.

The problem here was I didn't think this was really a records case.

Yes, there were records of the sale of the land and efforts to change the zoning– to prepare for that different outlet mall project in neighboring Bathport– and bank records to show that Michael's client had moved significant sums of money during the process.

But so what?

The client was a contractor with town hall connections and several projects in the works. The money could have come from anywhere.

Unless the prosecutors had someone who saw Todd hand a brick of cash to the zoning chief (and we would have known if they had) this was not going to be a slam dunk.

Not even close.

As daunting a task as the piles of paper were, they were actually encouraging. They meant the prosecutors weren't sure they could make it stick.

Which meant room for Michael to move.

Exactly what he needed.

I'd be happy to tell him that.

Whenever he finally got home.

In the meantime, there was a good doggie who needed walkies...and my own paid work to address.

At least Scotchie's easy.

CHAPTER 18
DOING THE SORT

By pickup time, I had a pretty good handle on the book proposal and the documents. And another cup of coffee under my belt, so I had a fighting chance.

At the library, Daniel and Cherise took off for the kids' room, and Corinna and I got down to it. My plan was to be as low-key as possible so I could see their reaction when I brought up an old book.

Ideally, with both Corinna and Moira in the room.

I got my shot ten minutes in, after Corinna and I had re-boxed all the paperback romances (who knew there were so many bodice-ripper fans– or so few cover designs: woman spilling out of dress as hot guy in half-unbuttoned puffy shirt nuzzles/menaces/embraces her.)

Moira poked her head in the doorframe. "How's it going?"

Corinna managed a nonchalant air. "Looks like it won't be too hard to put it all back up. Everything seems to be pretty much where it was when all hell broke loose."

"So we don't have to do the Big Sort again," I assured her. The Big Sort happens each year in the week before the sale. Donations are basically organized by genre as they come in, but only when we're getting ready for the sale do we move boxes into place and really track what we have. It's a very long afternoon.

"That is a relief." Moira nodded.

"Say," I started, keeping my voice as neutral as possible, "did either of you see a really old book in the box from Madge? She thinks she may have given away a family heirloom by accident."

Moira froze for just an instant.

"Oh, no!" Corinna said. "We'll give it back, of course."

"Um, of course." Moira spoke too quickly. "I think I saw a few things with those old embossed leather covers."

"This one was dark purple. It might have looked black," I said.

"I vaguely remember something like that," Moira replied. I recognized her careful tone because I'd just been doing the same thing.

"Oh, I saw it." Corinna shook her head. "I sold it."

"Oh, no." I didn't have to fake concern. "Who to?"

"Kryssie." Her eyes gleamed. "Said it was just the right color for the meditation table in her she-shed."

"She-shed?" I repeated. I wasn't sure I'd heard the word. I did know I'd never said it.

Moira giggled. "It's the latest thing, ladies. You've heard of man-caves, well, she-sheds are where our poor overworked housewives go to do self-care."

"You've got the language down," I said.

"I've heard it enough times from board members." Moira looked and sounded almost her normal self again. But there definitely had been a moment.

"Self-care." Corinna sighed. "I'm aware of the concept, I just can't imagine having a shed to do it in."

"Right? I'm grateful if I get twenty minutes for a long bath," I said.

We shared wistful sighs at the thought of having time, energy, and money for a she-shed.

"So anyway, Grace," Moira continued with just a tiny bit of

something off in her tone, "you should probably go after Miss She-Shed. You can probably get it back from her. It's not like she was reading it."

"I'm not a hundred percent sure she reads anything other than that insane PTA newsletter of hers," Corinna said.

"You mean the immortal prose of *Rollin' at Rowland*?" I snickered. "She asked if I could edit it, and I told her I had too many projects this fall."

"Because you are not actively insane," Corinna said. "We're already volunteering for the social and going to the monthly meetings."

"You two do more than your share," Moira pronounced. "Brian too. Poor guy's a soft touch."

"He is. Kryssie does that whole we are so glad you're here thing that would make him barf anywhere but his kid's school," Corinna said.

"But it *is* our kids' school, and we put up with a lot," I reminded her.

"Yeah." Moira looked a little bit wistful. "You do. It's part of the game. The things we do for family."

As we returned to work, and the conversation moved on, I couldn't help wondering what Moira had done, and why.

Thinking about family reminded me of Brian and Old Man Loquat, and after I scooped up Daniel, I swung by the hardware store just to make sure everyone was okay.

Old Man Loquat certainly was.

He was on the porch in a patch of sunshine with Jimmy Stewart on his lap.

"Hey, it's Gracie and the little fella!" he called, with a big bright smile.

Jimmy Stewart raised her head and shot Daniel and me a glare. But that was all. Unlike Connery, she was a basically placid and friendly cat. Which did make me wonder how Old Man Loquat upset her enough to get scratched.

"Hi, Mr. Loquat!" Daniel went over and shook hands, the way Michael had shown him.

Mr. Loquat grinned at me over his head, as he always did. "You're raising him right."

"His dad's the one who taught him that," I reminded him.

"You know, for a hired gun, that guy of yours is pretty good."

"He was a standup guy before he was a hired gun, and he still is."

"Can I go in and see if Zoey's around?" Daniel asked.

I nodded, and he sped away as I turned to Old Man Loquat. "How are you doing, sir?"

"Brian ratted, didn't he?" His face tightened into a scowl that would not have been out of place on Daniel.

"He did. You can't mess around with cat scratches. You know where those claws have been."

Old Man Loquat's scowl faded slightly. "Okay, that's fair. Wasn't that bad, anyhow. They cleaned it out, gave me some antibiotics, and sent a huge bill to Medicare. Gotta love modern medicine."

"Sure do." I looked at the cat still happily dozing in his lap. "How on earth did you get that sweet thing to claw you?"

A sheepish shrug. "Stepped on her tail. Straight-out accident, but she swiped at my ankle. I would have too."

I nodded. "Can't blame them when they're just defending themselves."

"Exactly." He stroked Jimmy Stewart. "Sometimes I like animals better than people."

"Yeah. I can understand that."

"How'd it go at the big town council woo hoo last night?"

"Not too bad. It was pretty much the Ginny Pescatore show, but that's better than everybody looking at me."

"Aw, c'mon, Gracie. You aren't shy, are you?"

"Not really. It just all felt weird to me."

"Don't blame you. Wasn't really about you."

"It sure wasn't." As always, I was impressed by Old Man Loquat's perception.

"Best thing you can do is stay out of that Ginny's way."

"Really?" I tried to sound interested, but not too eager.

"Really. Woman would sell her grandmother to get ahead politically. You know people talk about stuff here."

"Of course."

"And," he said with a grin like a little boy sneaking a cookie, "they say almost anything in front of me when I'm sitting out here because I'm just an old coot."

I had to stifle a laugh.

"It's okay, Gracie. I know that's how some folks think. Not you, not Brian– but some folks. So I hear stuff."

"And what did you hear about Ginny?"

"Well, here's the weird part. She was talking about her plans for running the council a week ago."

"A week ago?" I asked. "But Mrs. Winch was still-"

"Alive." He nodded. "Probably just big talk. She's one of those."

"That she is."

"They're really sure Obedellia died of natural causes, aren't they?" he asked.

"I think so. They wouldn't be having the calling hours tomorrow night if they weren't." While I was thrilled to have something else pointing to Ginny as a suspect, I sure didn't need Old Man Loquat playing detective.

Or anyone thinking he knew something about what they'd done. Add him to the list of people I have to protect.

"Well," he said, "then it's probably nothing. Just thinking about it now, it seems a little odd she was talking about what she'd do when she was running the place...and before you know it, she was."

"Coincidence." I said it as firmly as I could without making a big deal of it.

"You're right, Gracie. Been watching too much *Law & Order* again."

"Well, why not?" I sensed a good subject change. "Better than a lot of that new reality stuff."

"Isn't that the truth?" His expression suggested my gambit had worked. "Can you tell me why somebody thinks we want to watch a bunch of people fighting over food on a desert island? They did it better on *Gilligan's Island*– and at least that was fun."

"You're asking the wrong person. I don't get any of that."

"Don't get what?" Brian asked, walking out onto the porch, trailed by Zoey and Daniel. "Are we deploring the current state of men's clothes again?"

"No, whippersnapper," said Old Man Loquat with a teasing glance. "The state of television."

"Oh, we'll be here all night. And it's almost closing time."

"I have to stop at the grocery store anyhow– and a lot of work waiting at home," I said. "We're all too busy for that conversation."

"Save it for another day, Gracie. I've got plenty to say."

Bet he did.

CHAPTER 19
DOUBTS IN THE DAIRY AISLE

S ooner or later, most of Alcott turns up at the grocery store. The Super Duper is a top-of-the-line, state-of-the-art big, make that huge, box. It's on the same commercially zoned plot on the outskirts of town that the original store was grudgingly allotted in the 1950s, only with all the bells and whistles from a store designed to suck up all the disposable income of an upper-middle class suburb.

We have the organic section, every kind of meal kit you can imagine, a bakery and florist who could probably handle a royal wedding, and that's just the beginning. You get the idea.

It's lovely to have all of this, I suppose, but it does make it rather difficult to just run in and grab a gallon of milk, dog treats, and a packet of whatever cookies are on sale. Especially if you're traveling with a six-year-old.

If the store is a wonderland for grownups, it's a whole new dimension of magic for kids, with the lights and the signs and the big glass containers of cookies. And forget about the lobsters.

Daniel could spend all day watching the lobsters swim.

I haven't the heart to tell him what happens to the poor things.

So a quick grocery run is usually anything but. Think obstacle course slash aquarium with coupons.

Actually, since everyone in town comes through the place, make it obstacle course slash aquarium slash garden party.

The party started fast and early, in the expansive produce section. Kryssie Farrar was standing in the apple display, comparing Cortlandt and Mackintosh and studying her manicure, which as far as I could tell was the same beige as always, much like her cute little outfits. Today's was a plaid mini kilt with a cashmere t-shirt that probably cost more than my whole week's worth of clothes. I tried to pass quickly and invisibly, but I'd need actual paranormal abilities to escape her.

"Oh, Grace!" she trilled. "What a helpful coincidence!"

"Um, hi." I slowed down and got a dirty look from Daniel, who was looking forward to visiting his crustacean friends.

"Did you write the press release for the ice cream social?" she asked.

Somehow, I managed not to run her over with my cart and forced a smile. "I emailed it to you two weeks ago."

"Oh."

"I'll send it again." I'd written and sent the release as soon as I got home from drop-off right after she asked. Otherwise, I would have been caught flatfooted on a day just like today.

No, thanks.

"Thank you. Any chance you could-"

"Gotta go!" I pointed to Daniel who was drifting off in the direction of the lobsters. "A lot to do today."

Kryssie waggled a couple of fingers from one apple. I've never been so happy to be dismissed.

Daniel marched over to the lobster tank, drawn as if by a magnet.

"You haven't told him what they do with them, have you?"

I turned to see Al, watching Daniel with a warm gaze that suggested he had a small person in his life too.

"No way," I said.

"Good. Let 'em be kids as long as you can. He's six, right?"

"Yep."

"My granddaughters are too. Just adorable."

"I'm told it doesn't last. Corinna has a thirteen-year-old."

"Teenagers are pretty scary." He sighed. "But as long as you make sure they know they're loved– and where the lines are– it all washes out."

"Good to know."

Al gave me that little head shake that suggested he wanted to talk about our top-secret project, the ring for Madge. "Find anything nice?"

"Got a few ideas. Going to send you pics tonight."

A big happy smile. "Good. Thank you."

"It's fun for me."

"Hoping it'll be fun for me too." His smile faded a little. "She's acting kind of weird. I'm just a tiny bit worried."

"I think she's got a couple of really stressful cases right now. I don't know the details either, but I'm sure it doesn't have anything to do with you." I was actually pretty proud of myself for coming up with that.

Gave him the sense that something was up– and that it wasn't him. And even better, by referring to clients, that made it a confidential matter she couldn't discuss. Pretty slick for just spinning something up in the seafood section.

His face relaxed. "So maybe give her a little space?"

"It's going to take some time for that ring to get here. Let things work for now."

"Pretty good advice."

"Madge has told me the same thing about other stuff any number of times." I grinned.

"Nice. I've got to get these scallops home."

"And I've got to get him away from the tank before anything happens." I nodded to the seafood clerk moving toward the tank. "This is right up there with Santa and the Easter Bunny."

"No kidding. Pics tonight?"

"Tonight." We shared a quick hug, and I turned to Daniel. "C'mon buddy, we need to get that Fakin' Bacon, or Scotchie will never forgive us."

"Bye, lobsters!"

It was probably rude not to have Daniel greet Al, but at this point, it was more important to get him away from the tank before the clerk got there. The Super Duper sells lobsters both live and steamed, and I didn't want any awkward questions, or worse for him to see them scooped up for the pot.

After picking up the extra-large size of Fakin' Bacon for extra-large dogs, Daniel and I agreed on the chocolate and caramel flavors of the sandwich cookies on the two-for-the-price-of-one special. We were in the dairy aisle, and just a gallon of milk from the checkout and escape when we ran into yet another obstacle.

"Why, Grace Adair. How nice to see you here."

I recognized the voice. Not that nice.

George Germain, two cases down in yogurt, comparing organic Greek and coconut-milk varieties. His graying ponytail oozed from his receding hairline back over the collar of his mold-colored Patagonia fleece.

"Hi."

He looked at the half-gallon of two-percent in my hand. "Do you really feed that precious boy milk from hormone-treated cows? Aren't you afraid of what it will do to his testicles?"

It's fair to say I hadn't thought about Daniel's boy parts since potty training had freed me from cleaning them. It's also fair to say that Super Duper buys its milk from a hormone-free farmers' cooperative, like many stores in New England, and I'd done my research.

I put the milk in the cart.

"Well, you know Super Duper's house brand comes from the Limestone Mountain Cooperative, right?"

"Really?" George said, his eyes widening a little. "I didn't know that."

"Yeah. I don't always have time to do my research, but when I can, I do."

"Good for you, Grace." His tone was impressively patronizing. "Was nice to be able to honor you and Corinna last night."

"Thanks. Really not necessary." I shrugged. "It's what any decent person would do."

"Obedellia Winch was not a decent person." George Germain's eyes took on a nasty gleam. "She was doing her best to bring down this town."

"It didn't matter in the moment."

"Of course. Not to you two." There was something off in his tone.

"But it was very kind of the council to honor us– and I was glad to see the praise for the rescue squad too." I was trying to bring it back to some normal footing.

"We were glad to. Though we probably wouldn't have been if she'd made it."

My eyes widened a little.

"Not to be unkind, Grace, but nobody is sorry that woman is dead."

"Oh."

"Don't look so shocked. Honesty's the sunshine that kills evil. If we were all straightforward about our motivations, it would be a much better world."

"Um, sure." I patted Daniel's head. "Of course, lying is bad."

"So is bigotry, prejudice, and capricious budget-cutting," the councilman said, the gleam in his eyes edging toward fanatic. "Sooner or later, someone would have killed her just on sheer principle."

"Um, sure." I reached for my keys and the store card. "Well, we weren't worrying about what kind of person she was."

"I know. And that's very noble of both of you. Especially Corinna, considering all of the awful things that Winch woman tried to do to the library."

I let the keys rattle in my fingers.

"That heart attack was karma, believe you me," George Germain continued. "Never thought I'd be grateful to factory farms, chemicals, and the sedentary American lifestyle."

"I'm sure it's very sad for her family," I offered.

"Hah. That fool Morton is probably happiest of all to see her gone. I hear he had a side piece at town hall."

"None of my business," I said, keeping my tone as cool as possible. Not only was that a true and perfect statement of fact, it might also be a way to back George off.

"None of anybody's business, except that Morton was always sniffing around town hall acting like he was a councilman too. Figured he was one of those religious nuts who thinks everything his wife does is for him."

I nodded since he was finally offering useful information.

"'Course you're one of those little mamas too, aren't you?"

"What?"

"Well, didn't you give up a real job to stay at home with the kid?" He gave me the same dismissive look I'd seen from Ginny and any number of others. "It's not what women fought for, you know."

"I marched," I said quietly. Not often, but for a few things that really counted, you bet I had. "And we were, and are, fighting for choices, and a safe world to make them in. I don't get to tell other people how to organize their lives, and they don't get to tell me how to organize mine."

George Germain gave me the same stunned look I'd seen on Ginny the other day. I'm getting pretty bored with people looking at me like I'm a talking cat.

"Sorry, Grace. I didn't mean..."

"Never mind. Let's just chalk it up to a tense day and move on," I said. "I have to get home and work on some documents before dinner."

I could feel George Germain staring at me as I gathered up Daniel and headed for the front.

My cheeks were burning, and I'm sure I was blushing like a

volcano. I'd gone a lot harder than I should have, but that guy earned it.

Well, he hadn't really. He'd only done what any number of other people had, just at a time when I'd pretty well had enough.

It was only on the way home, as Daniel played with his constitutionally guaranteed Hot Wheels from the checkout, that I replayed the conversation and realized I'd missed something very important in the middle of my annoyance.

George Germain really hated Mrs. Winch. Enough to say openly he was glad she was dead.

I couldn't help wondering if he'd made her that way.

He hung around at the library too. He certainly would have had access to the organic materials used in the poison.

Means, motive, and opportunity.

The only question was whether he would actually do it.

That was a more complex issue than it sounds, which I knew better than anyone. Just because you can make the poison and have a good reason to use it (you believe) does not mean you're capable of that last step.

I didn't know for sure I was until my first commission.

Professor Munroe, I'm sure, knew all along.

It wasn't something people just gave off on the street though. And I honestly wasn't a hundred percent sure what to look for, despite a fair amount of experience with murderers in my prosecuting days.

What I could say with a decent degree of confidence was that George Germain could not be ruled out as a possible suspect. Which only added to the fun.

Like we didn't have enough already.

CHAPTER 20
BREAK THESE CHAINS
(OF CUSTODY)

Back at home, I put a casserole in the oven and took Daniel and Scotchie out for a walk, which gave me a chance to enjoy the pretty fall afternoon…and to think about everything I learned today.

I had part of a chain of custody: it went from Madge's basement to Al, to the library, and ultimately to Kryssie's she-shed.

She-shed, for heaven's sake.

But there was still a big gap in the middle, and I was pretty sure that whoever made and used the poison did it in that space. Which probably meant someone at the library.

Not necessarily someone *from* the library, but probably someone in the building.

Scotchie attempted to chase every squirrel he smelled, never mind saw, so it wasn't as much we went for a walk as that he took us. Still, considering the possibility blue doggie doo from the latest slurp of poster paint was still hanging over our heads (metaphorically only, thankfully) I was happy to walk him as much as necessary.

Daniel always liked watching Scotchie sniff for squirrels and try to get away, so I got the joy of hearing that wonderful little boy giggle that bubbles up from somewhere in his toes.

I'm going to miss that when he gets older.

That was a worry for another day though.

Right now, I was absolutely convinced Moira was holding something back. Her initial reaction to my question about the Book, and the way she spoke so carefully to Corinna and me meant only one thing.

Guilt.

The problem is guilt looks the same no matter what you're feeling guilty about.

From there, it's a matter of degree, and that's unique to each person.

Moira could be feeling guilty because she saw the poison recipe and thought about it...or she could really be the person who used it to put Obedellia Winch out of our misery.

I didn't know her well enough to know how much it would take to get the guilt response. Only that something to do with the Book had. It would be just as dangerous to assume she was the one who compounded and used the poison as to assume she wasn't.

All I knew for sure was she was guilty about something and she was lying– and not comfortable with it.

That wasn't a negative. Good people aren't supposed to be comfortable with lying. I'm only comfortable lying in the direct service of a commission, and even then, they're usually minor half-truths, like an errand in New York that is only part of the reason for the trip.

What I've had to do is get comfortable with a larger sort of deception. People assume I am one thing, and indeed I am. But I'm also something else, and if they knew, they'd find it disturbing, at the very least.

There's an awful lot of work associated with keeping the secret every day.

And the sheer weight of carrying it.

Carrying *them*.

I'm not going to tell you my number, but I've been doing this once or twice a year since the end of law school, so it is not small. A few years ago, when that very famous former FBI chief was talking up his book, he was on the Sunday night news show talking about mobsters and how their first kill is difficult, and it gets easier from there.

I had to hide my explosive– and incredulous– laugh from Michael.

Maybe it's easy for mob guys.

It's never easy for us, and we wouldn't want it to be. Part of the reason we've been able to do this in secret for several centuries is we do it with absolute awareness of the seriousness of what we're doing. We are, in fact, taking the power of life and death onto ourselves, with the nominal and unseen guidance of the Archangel.

Not a small lift, especially for a bunch of nice ladies.

As it should be.

I suspect, though Professor Munroe never confirmed this to me, that one of the things the Mothers look for in prospective sisters is a very strong ethical code, almost to the point of inflexibility. If you're going to be playing God, you'd better know where your lines are.

None of which prevents us from feeling guilt.

I know of a few sisters who regularly confess to infidelity to their priests to get absolution and some measure of spiritual comfort. Their logic is simple: a mortal sin is a mortal sin, so it's close enough.

I don't think God plays horseshoes, and I'd rather risk eternal damnation than have anyone think I would cheat on Michael.

Besides, the way I understand it, the Archangel will intercede for us when the time comes. I'm not going to judge my sisters for getting comfort any way they can find it (within the bounds of our vows) but it's not for me.

"SCOTCHIE! NO!" Daniel's shout at the dog brought me back.

Scotchie was sniffing at something that might once have been a squirrel, but was now just a few bits of fur and bone, probably day or two old roadkill. Ugh.

"Scotchie!" I snapped. "That's not for you."

He backed off and gave me the sad puppy eyes. Probably, he really was upset he'd offended his humans. But it's also his best weapon, and I'm never sure if he's working me.

"It's okay, pal," I said, petting him.

"We love you, Scotchie," Daniel added, leaning in for a lick.

Great. Now I was going to have to spray them both down with disinfectant.

"C'mon, guys, let's head home for a good wash."

"Do I hafta?" Daniel asked.

"Yes, you *have to* wash."

Daniel grumbled. Michael and I are both sticklers for diction. To have any hope of success with juries, I'd had to lose a Western PA accent, and Michael had to get rid of his New York tendency to talk way too fast. We're probably overly picky, but it's a lot easier to grow up with a good, clean delivery than to learn one as an adult.

With squirrel germ removal now on the program, we turned for home. Scotchie hauling me along, clearly hoping that there might be some Fakin' Bacon back at the house.

At least we'd be able to fix this one with treats and antibacterial soap.

The situation with Moira was a lot tougher.

I didn't really think she'd coldly poison Mrs. Winch. Without the apprenticeship and support of the sisterhood, I don't think most people are capable of that sort of thing.

But people are capable of an awful lot if they believe their life, or the way they live, is threatened. Or if they believe someone they love is at risk. Or both.

Moira's mother was in that expensive dementia care place, and as far as I knew, she didn't have many resources beyond her town employee's salary. I don't know what her parents had done for a living, and there might have been a nice pension or health plan helping out in there, but maybe not too.

If she thought she was going to be fired or, more likely, forced into early retirement by Mrs. Winch's budget cuts...

Even a nice librarian might be capable of poisoning.

There was one bright spot here though.

After our conversation, I was absolutely certain Corinna had nothing to do with the Book, or its use. I knew her well enough to know she wasn't holding back or diverting my attention.

I'd always thought she was more likely to help Moira cover her tracks than to actually harm Mrs. Winch. She didn't like the council chair any more than the rest of us did, but there was no murder-level animosity there.

Yes, people sometimes kill for stupid reasons, but usually there's something else involved making them stupid. As in drugs, alcohol, or sex, all of which can make the most rational person do dumb things. Just ask Michael.

And then there was time.

Even if Corinna wanted to poison Mrs. Winch, she just would not have had the time to do it. I have to work very carefully around everything in my life to make the subtle poison, and I know exactly how to do it and how long it takes.

A woman who's juggling a cranky teen, a six-year-old, and a full-time job would simply never be able to do it for the first time. It took me a week to make the first batch, and I was a single law student.

Corinna should have been in the clear all along.

But not Moira.

Moira was always the best bet.

I didn't like the idea of either of my close friends as a killer. And I really didn't like what might happen from here.

"Mom! Look!" Daniel's shout brought me back.

"What?" I asked, blinking and shaking my head a little.

"Look what Scotchie did!"

He pointed, giggling. The dog gave us both a sheepish expression.

"Well," I said, putting Scotchie's head, "we don't have to worry about that poster paint anymore."

It's not good when Blue Doo Part Two is the highlight of your day.

CHAPTER 21
DANCING DOWN
MEMORY LANE

M ichael arrived just in time for dinner– Mexican lasagna, a simple and delicious masterpiece of cultural appropriation– loaded the dishwasher, and crashed on the couch with Daniel, Scotchie, and the old sitcom about two prissy psychologists on the streaming channel.

With the fellas busy, I actually got an hour to work on the book proposal and felt almost pleased with the direction of the thing by bedtime. Daniel and Scotchie's bedtime, that is.

After boy and dog were settled for the night, and the big one reluctantly back in his office, I treated myself to a glass of wine and a much happier task.

Rings.

With the happy knowledge I could get the Book back from Kryssie, I was feeling optimistic enough to see if I could find a suitable band for Al to offer Madge. Oh, I knew she was probably still every bit as unwilling to accept it as she'd been a day ago.

But what you think you want and what you actually do when life offers you something else are not necessarily the same thing.

I should know.

A dozen or so years ago, I'd been certain I would be a career prosecutor. Maybe state's attorney one day, or maybe a bureau chief for the Feds if I got a really lucky break. No question I was about the work.

It started to change that summer night at Swing on the Green, when the big redheaded guy I'd seen around the law library came over and asked if I knew how to lindy.

As it happened, I still had a few moves left over from college theatre, and I'd never had such a good partner. We danced till the band packed up, then spent hours talking over cinnamon toast at a nearby diner.

The date ended at my door the next morning.

We were unofficially engaged within a month, married in six.

Still, even then, I had no doubt I belonged in the courtroom.

I figured we'd have a kid or two, and they'd go to some excellent preschool, and I'd continue my much more important life. And, of course, my other work.

Then I got pregnant.

Pregnancy is more than a little fraught for someone who handles poison on a regular basis. Sure, seven hundred years' worth of other sisters had safely carried to term. Once you've built a poison tolerance, it's not an issue. Still, it's one thing to know that in your head, and another entirely to feel it in your body.

It was a lot more than that though.

By then, I'd taken life enough times I wasn't sure I would be allowed to give it.

Doesn't make sense, of course. We've signed on for a mission from the Archangel, and we know we're doing the right thing. No reason to fear any sort of divine punishment.

Still, though, when the nurses handed me that little redheaded bundle, everything changed. I looked down into blue-violet eyes like mine, and he owned me.

Owned Michael, too.

And there was no way I was going to give up any second I could have with him if I could avoid it.

Sure, looking back with almost seven years of perspective, a lot of it was hormones. And if Michael didn't push me to stay at home, he certainly didn't fight me. Daniel was maybe a week old when Michael came out of his office saying he'd run the numbers. His solo practice was really starting to take off, and the cost of childcare and commuting to New Haven would take up most of my assistant state's attorney salary anyway.

I could stay with Daniel for a year if I wanted.

It wasn't just money, of course.

One year became six, and eventually, I started the editing and fact-checking business to have a little something of my own. But Daniel has been my main job since he was born, and I don't regret it at all.

Pretty much the last thing I'd have imagined when I was in law school.

So I wasn't really taking Madge's insistence she didn't want to marry Al at face value. I suspected some of it was the situation with the Book, some of it was her late husband, and some of it was fear of a new loss. With that in mind, I had to believe if Al walked in with a lovely ring once this mess was safely over, she might well see things differently.

It was my job to find that lovely ring.

One of my favorite magazines has a wonderful online shopping advice section, and a few months ago, they ran an article on new fine-jewelry designs. A couple of companies caught my eye then, and I started there.

Goldflower, a woman-owned brand with designs inspired by nature, has one of those nice websites with the slide show on the front page, displaying their best necklaces, rings, and bracelets. I was just getting ready to click on the "Rings" page when I saw it.

A delicate white-metal chain, with a flower charm, covered in light-pink and dark-pink stones. The bracelet I found in the library parking lot that Morton Winch had claimed. And the same bracelet I saw on the woman in the zoning office yesterday.

Really?

I clicked on the picture.

It was part of the Shimmering Blossoms Collection, and a really high-end piece. White gold with pink topaz and rubellite. Several hundred dollars, even with the Fall Fantasy discount code.

That's why he wanted it back, obviously. The Book wasn't the only thing that went flying when Mrs. Winch fell. But what was she doing with it?

And why did Morton Winch give it to the woman in zoning?

She was small, blonde, and pretty in that very 'done' suburban way. So, the last question was fairly easy to answer. Was I being unkind if I suspected she was tolerating him because he gave her things like that bracelet?

Maybe.

But, I realized, I'm back to chain of custody. The only real way the bracelet could have ended up just lying in the library parking lot is if it came there with Mrs. Winch. If she had it on her somewhere. There were only a few ways that could happen, and none of them were good for Morton Winch.

Before the bracelet, I'd thought he had a vague motive to kill her: she was a deeply unpleasant human to everyone in town, and *we* didn't have to wake up with her. This, though, gave him a very specific reason to want her dead.

Want her dead and want the path cleared.

And if she had the bracelet, she knew he was up to dirty.

No reasonable person would think Obedellia Winch would wear that piece.

She'd realize that the second she laid eyes on it.

Devil's Advocate: no reasonable person would look at me and see Tweety Bird's big blue eyes, but Michael does. Love isn't reasonable.

No, but it's not blind, deaf, and completely detached from reality either.

Usually.

But the couples who see each other as magical love objects in defiance of all logic treat each other a certain way. It's usually obvious to everyone around them, or at least shows in flashes. Not even a glimmer with the Winches.

That bracelet could not have been meant for her.

And she would have known it.

She would also have known it was expensive. I doubted she spent any time surfing fine jewelry sites for fun, but the quality of the craftsmanship, and the sparkle of the stones made it clear it wasn't just a junky costume piece.

Smart money is always on the husband.

There was still one very big problem with this picture. I could not put the poison in his hands. I knew the Book had made it to the library, and I knew the poison was used on Mrs. Winch there...but that was it.

If– big if– he was the one who did it, he had to have gotten the Book. And then have made the subtle poison, no small hurdle in itself.

On the other hand, just because you can't figure out how something happened doesn't mean it didn't happen.

At the very least, we suddenly had another very good suspect.

And I'd be seeing him at the calling hours tomorrow night.

There was at least a possibility I might finally be getting somewhere with this.

Or not.

I clicked on the "Rings" tab. Al needed some good ideas. I sure hoped he was going to need them.

As I closed my laptop after sending off the pics, a glass of wine materialized in front of me.

"Thought you might need this as much as I do."

Michael sat down beside me and clinked. "Long day at the ranch."

"Yep." I took a sip. "How's it going?"

"You saw the document list. It's not. It's like being in the middle of a blizzard, only you're expected to catalogue every snowflake."

"That's deliberate, I'm sure."

"That much, I knew." He drank a bit of his wine. "They're making a records case and-"

"But it's not a records case."

He put down the wine. "Tell me."

"It's been a while since I've gone to trial, but to win a real records case, you need documents showing each element along the way, right? They filed this report, then that form, then made this representation, and so on."

"Right. That's why they're drowning us in documents."

"And that's fine. But some elements of the crime won't show up in the records. They can prove your client had a project in the works, and that he withdrew cash, but they can't have records showing him putting money in the hands of a town official."

"That's true. I've been looking for some kind of deposit record. The official in Bathport is cooperating, so I expected to see something from him."

"And you haven't."

"Not so far."

"That means something."

Michael smiled and picked his up his glass. "You're right, it does."

"I need to look through things some more, but I'm getting a theory. I'm starting to think they're drowning you in records because they're hoping you'll miss things."

"Really?"

"There's more to it than that. But would it be consistent? Throw everything at you in the hopes you won't have the energy to sift through it?"

"Especially since it's me, and not a big firm."

"Right. A firm can put tons of associates on this. You've got two clerks, and Annie."

"And you."

"Well, yes, and me." I smiled at him over my glass. "Consider me your secret weapon."

"Something like that." He drank another sip and contemplated. "So you figure they're trying to scare me into submission with the document dumps. Coming in hard like it's a records case to make me convince my client to plead to the top charge because he can't win."

"I think there's at least a possibility."

"Do you think they have much of a case in the middle of all that?"

"I don't know, honestly. One of us needs to look at everything they're sending us and see what's really there. And what's not."

"If they have a smoking gun."

"Or if they're just throwing smoke." I nodded.

"Think you can do that in between everything else?"

"I can make a start. I've got the book proposal marked up, so I need to put some time in on it tomorrow...but I should be able to get at least enough time to get a look."

"Sounds good. I'll work on things from my end– see if I can find out the disposition of some recent major corruption cases."

"I still have a few friends in the State's Attorney's Office, and an old Penn State classmate of mine is over at the Feds now."

"You mean Marisol?"

"Yeah. Remember, she moved up here for the schools? Her kids were in preschool in Brooklyn, but she couldn't afford the private school fees in the city. She's deputy chief in the white-collar bureau in New Haven, and her kids are in Woodbridge."

"Better public schools there than a lot of private ones." Michael's contemplative expression reminded me that we'd considered Woodbridge.

"Exactly. I'm kind of her Connecticut mom life expert. She'll give me a few minutes."

"Would you mind calling her tomorrow?"

"Be nice to talk to someone who's still in the game."

Michael drank the last of his wine. "Want to go watch bad TV in bed?"

"Sounds like a plan."

"What an exciting married life we have," he said.

I drained my glass. "We could do a lot worse."

CHAPTER 22
FROM THE DROP

B rian was waiting with Zoey and coffee when Corinna and I walked up with our kids the next morning.

A real treat and badly needed. Once again, I'd been scrambling all morning; everything seemed to take extra time, and nothing suited Daniel. Or Scotchie, who'd managed to be even more underfoot than usual, a significant achievement for a giant blond dog.

Michael? He left early to start working on the documents. I understood it, but I can't say I appreciated it.

It's fair to say I allowed myself a little low-grade cursing as I threw a big gray sweater over my leggings and checked to make sure I had matching shoes, if nothing else coordinated.

Corinna wasn't doing much better. She had a frazzled expression even before Cherise dropped her lunchbox, sending little square plastic containers skidding all over the sidewalk. They were cute– clear with bright blue lids, probably one of those fancy sets they sell on the shopping channels.

Daniel, Zoey, and I jumped in to help scoop them up, and thankfully none popped open. Brian, whose hands were full of good coffee, looked a little guilty. But we didn't need five people to pick up four containers.

"At least these don't explode like the cheaper ones do," Corinna said as she re-packed the bag.

"They are nice and sturdy. The shopping channel ones?" I asked.

"Clay was watching and decided to make our storage more efficient. Whatever makes him happy."

We shared knowing glances about our men, and the way they try to organize us, on the way to Brian who held out the go-tray from Louisa's.

"What's this?" I asked.

"Just my little way of saying thank you for covering yesterday while I took my great-uncle to the urgent care."

"Not necessary," I said.

"Not even a little," Corinna agreed. "But kind."

"And desperately needed," I added, taking a deep sniff of the wonderful rich roast. "How is it possible Louisa's coffee is so much better than anyone else's?"

"They buy good stuff and prepare it carefully." Brian happily took a sip from his cup. "They love what they do, and it shows."

"Yep." Corinna got a whiff of hers. "Good stuff. If you're where you want to be, doing what you're supposed to be doing, nothing is really work."

"Like say, scooping up books left all over the reading area?" I asked with a teasing smile.

"Pretty much." She took a sip of coffee. "I'm not going to get all gooey here but working at the library was worth every lousy job and boring course it took to get there."

"Don't tell Old Man Loquat, but I feel pretty much the same about the store." Brian gave us a sheepish grin.

"We already knew that." I toasted him with my cup.

"Now we just have to find something more fulfilling for you, Grace," Corinna said.

I stared for a second. My secret vocation is very fulfilling in its way, but it doesn't take up a lot of time in my life. And the editing work was just something to do until Daniel was older and I could return to law…wasn't it?

I was stunned to realize I hadn't really thought that through.

"I'm so fulfilled I don't know what day it is," I said, trying to play it off.

"You need to be back in a courtroom, and you know it." Corinna's tone was matter of fact, but affectionate. "You know, we could figure out some kind of schedule, so you have some backup if you start doing legal work again."

I nodded. "Been thinking about pitching in with Michael once in a while."

"You should," Brian urged. "Bet you're fire in court."

"I was." I shrugged. "Different world– different life."

"Never know. Things cycle around," Corinna said.

"They do, at that." I drank a bit more coffee. "Today, though, the only cycle we need to worry about is the life cycle. I'm not going into those calling hours alone."

Corinna scowled. "I know we have to go."

"I want to go," Brian said.

"Why on earth?" Corinna said it, but I thought it too.

"Because I want to be sure she's dead. After everything she put this town through– and especially after that stupid snowman donnybrook, I want to watch 'em drag her out."

A little vengeful for our normally sweet Brian.

Corinna and I looked sharply at him.

"That stupid drag queen thing that came up at the beginning of the council meeting earlier this week? She started it and got the Brewer guy on board. And at least once when she was visiting the store, she looked at Zoey and me and asked if she was my daughter…or what?"

We stared. Even Obedellia Winch should not have been capable of that level of rudeness in 2023 in Connecticut.

"Yeah. Made some comment about how kids need a mom and a dad."

"I'm sorry, honey." Corinna patted his arm.

"Horrid," I agreed. "You can't fix stupid."

"I know, and I sure didn't like knowing she was out there threatening everything Zoey and I are trying to build in this place. After Jamie..."

I put a hand on his other arm. It probably looked like we were having some kind of group hug thing, but who cares? Brian needed comfort and support. That's the whole point of having friends.

Brian took a breath, the bell rang, and the moment passed.

It was only in my car I started wondering how far Brian might go to stop Mrs. Winch. If she was a threat to the life he'd built...he could have seen the Book too.

One more thing I didn't want to think about.

CHAPTER 23
THE BOOK DEAL

My phone rang as I pulled out of the Rowland lot.

Unfamiliar number.

Could have been spam, but I was willing to bet the farm it wasn't.

"Grace, dear."

Professor Munroe.

"Hello, Professor."

"How are matters proceeding?"

"Reasonably well," I said, hoping I sounded sincere. "I should have the Book in my hands very soon."

"And the person who used the recipe?"

"They'll be in hand soon as well. I'm assuming the preference is to convince them to stay silent rather than to remove them?" I asked hopefully.

"You know, Grace, we never endorse unnecessary taking of life."

"I do." Whew. Still room to move. "That's why I'm hoping to settle this without any further harm."

"Good girl. Do you have a plan?"

"I'm getting there. Let's just say there are a number of people who will keep their silence in order to buy mine.

A very dry reply: "Blackmail is a beautiful thing."

"It is indeed."

"And a good bit less painful than other means."

"True, Professor." I took a breath. "We have until Saturday, correct?"

"Saturday brunch, but of course the sooner the better."

"Of course. We will send you a picture of the burning Book when we have it."

"I do hate burning books, Grace."

"So do I. But there's no choice."

"Sadly, none at all. Margaret told me what poor Eliza had done. There was definitely a certain lapse in supervision."

Which meant we never should have been in this position.

Not much consolation since we were here now.

"We're putting things right, Professor."

"I have no doubt you're doing all you can. I have great confidence in you, Grace, I always have."

Not the worst way to end a call with your mentor.

Professor Munroe had been a revelation to me. Growing up in rural Western Pennsylvania, the daughter of a single mother before that was cool, I didn't have any doubt women could support themselves and their families.

But I didn't understand they could have callings.

My mother, a teacher and later a vice-principal, had a job. She was committed to her work and took pride in it, but she didn't define herself as a professional the way Professor Munroe, a respected former prosecutor and legal scholar, had.

I was always the smartest kid in the classroom in my small factory town, and when I won a scholarship to Penn State, I had a lot of drive, but wasn't sure what to do with it. I was leaning toward teaching myself until Professor Munroe spoke to my junior-year women's history seminar. As she explained four centuries of jurisprudence, and women's place in it, I was hooked.

And awed by the Professor. It was truly the moment when I knew who, and what, I wanted to be when I grew up.

I applied for, and won, a law scholarship.

Law school is when I really got to know Professor Munroe, and ultimately, when she chose me. It wasn't that she was like a mother to me, though my mother died the summer between undergrad and law school. She was the cool aunt who showed you the kind of life you could make for yourself– if you were smart and brave enough.

You've probably been wondering why I joined.

Maybe thinking there's some kind of pathology, some violation, some predator in my background who made me want to become an avenging angel, for lack of a better description.

Sorry to disappoint you. I have a few daddy issues, since mine left when I was a toddler and died soon afterwards in a depressingly normal car crash. But my grandfather and uncle were good men. Standup guys, as Michael would say. Uncle Frank gave me away at our wedding and still stays in touch from California.

So no, this isn't personal in any direct sense.

It *is* personal in the sense the need to remove evil men from the world is everybody's business. I'm not in charge of who is chosen as a sister, but I suspect they deliberately stay away from actual survivors of abuse. There would be an extremely powerful temptation to put the power to use to settle your own scores rather than those you're given.

I guess I was pretty much the ideal candidate: smart, driven, ethical– and without either a problematic history, or too much close family.

There's also the simple fact I turned out to be very good at it.

Professor Munroe, I'm sure, saw that all along.

I didn't know until my first commission, the owner of a large regional electronics store chain who fleeced customers in his shops and engaged in far more damaging predation with young female relatives at home. One of them decided it was time to stop him, and I was chosen to do it.

The whole thing was surprisingly straightforward, but not easy.

All it took was a touch on the arm to apply the poison in the midst of a very intense conversation about a junky television I would have been paying for long after it broke.

That first time, I shook for hours sure that a couple of Pennsylvania State Troopers would show up at my little college apartment and drag me away. Finally started making fudge that night to have something to do. Maybe something to bribe the cops.

Of course, it didn't work out that way.

But the fudge is still my self-soothing thing.

I had one more thing to do before I could go home and get to work. Pay our PTA princess a little visit and get the Book out of her she-shed.

The Newsome Realty office is in a corner of The Plaza, between a nail salon and the big grocery store. At least I knew why Kryssie's manicure is always perfect.

She looked up when I walked in, giving me a perky, and thoroughly fake, smile. "Grace! Do you have questions about the social tomorrow night?"

"No. I have questions about a book you bought at the fair."

"What book?"

Don't make a big deal, I reminded myself. I know it's life or death, but she doesn't. "An old one. Corinna said you bought it for the she-shed. It's a family piece Madge gave away by accident."

"But I like it. It's pretty."

"It's important to Madge. We'll pay what you paid, of course."

"Is it valuable?"

"Not especially. It's just a family piece that matters a lot to Madge."

"Really?" Her bright little eyes assessed me. Like a lot of manipulators, she wasn't all that smart, but she was very canny.

"Really. You don't need to worry about that." I gave her the look. The one I almost never use in normal society. The one that was the last sight of the world for my assignments. Intensity dialed down just slightly because I didn't need her fainting on me.

"Well, then…I guess if it matters to you-" she sputtered.

I smiled. Friendly, harmless. She didn't really see that, did she? "I'll pay you what you paid."

"Fifty bucks."

"It was twenty. I helped set up the fair, remember?" Even the oldest books weren't more than twenty. We didn't think it was right to overcharge. And she would have been more suspicious if I hadn't argued about the price. That's how she's wired.

"Oh, fine. I'll bring it to the social tomorrow night."

"Please do." I let a little of the cold creep back into my gaze. "Don't forget."

Kryssie swallowed. Picked up her water bottle. "Don't worry, I won't."

You bet she won't.

I was starting to feel just a little optimistic as I drove home.

From the car, I called the U.S. Attorney's Office and left a message for my old pal Marisol. She'd probably get back to me after morning meetings.

Things got better at the house. A regular client asked me if I had time to go over her next manuscript, and we worked out a schedule. Since it was a full manuscript, that meant a fair amount of work, and noticeable cash. Not bad.

I was just getting ready to return to the 19th century poisoning book proposal when Marisol called back.

"How go the Mommy Wars?"

"PTA ice cream social tomorrow night."

"You win." She laughed, a wonderful rich sound that would have shocked juries used to her almost dour on-duty presentation. Marisol is one of those women who is gray flannel and business at work, and denim and goofy tees on her own time. "I've got family book club."

"Works for me."

"Maybe. Janna's still not too sure about suburbia. But we weren't the only same-sex couple at the open house, so…"

"Told you you'd like Woodbridge."

"It's surprisingly okay. Definitely a big adjustment from Brooklyn, but not bad."

Marisol and Janna Ruiz-Miller were the happy thoroughly undramatic parents of adorable twin kindergartners. They both had some entirely reasonable concerns about New England and suburbia, and I was glad to know things were going well. "Excellent."

"How are you and the wild Scotsman?" The question came with affectionate irony. Marisol thought (not entirely without reason) that Michael looked a bit like the guy in *Outlander*.

"Not bad, if the Scotsman weren't tearing his hair out over his big corruption case."

"He's not defending the Bathport guy, is he?"

"Yep. Why?"

Marisol sighed. "Let's just say some folks will not be happy to know a good guy like Michael Adair is involved in this."

"Oh?" At least partial confirmation of my theory.

"I would not have advised going to trial with one defendant when there is a pattern of bad behavior and cases against at least a couple co-conspirators that were not yet ripe. We only get one shot, after all."

"Yep. Makes sense with the way this one is going. They're drowning him in paper." Not talking out of school, just old friends commiserating.

"I would too. They should have waited until they nailed down the Alcott part of the case."

"There's an Alcott part of the case?"

"I've probably said too much already." Marisol took a long

breath, clearly thinking what to say. "Look, tell Michael to keep his eyes open, and if any of his client's friends want to talk, to send them my way."

Friends as in co-conspirators, I knew she meant. "Will do."

"All right," she said in a much lighter tone. "Now you're going to tell me about the ice cream, because they don't serve refreshments at the book club."

"No cookies?"

"Not one, can you believe it?"

"Well, that's just a crime against nature..."

CHAPTER 24
TO THE FAITHFUL (?) DEPARTED

While I was feeling pretty optimistic about the Book and Michael's case by pickup time, it's fair to say I wasn't feeling the love when we got to Mrs. Winch's calling hours.

It made sense for the three of us to just head over after pickup, so I neatened myself up and met Corinna and Brian at Rowland, with plans to drop our cars at the hardware store since it was very close to Spring's Funeral Home.

We parked the kids with Mr. Loquat, who was more than happy to allow Imani to think she was in charge of the younger ones. Old Man Loquat, and the long-lamented Mrs. Loquat, had raised three daughters and a son, and he had some kind of special radar for Imani, who was fractious with almost everyone else.

"She's the same with my grandfather," Corinna told Brian and me as we walked the short distance to the funeral home. "They're old enough to command respect, but distant enough she doesn't think they're bossing her. I'm thinking of sending her to Granddad until she's thirty."

We laughed.

It was a joke, but not a joke, the way parental humor often is.

And it was the last fun moment for a while.

The calling hours were a must-do for most of the town.

Spring's Funeral Home (with a name that was a built-in irony alert) has been burying folks in New Haven County for the better part of a century and a half. Unfortunately, the original Victorian house location is two towns over. The Alcott location is a thoroughly hideous mid-20th century brick box. It could be a medical office or an insurance agency.

Which, again, I know, irony alert.

We all tensed as we got to the door, for different reasons. Brian, of course, was having flashbacks to his husband's death. For Corinna, it was her dad and grandmother. Me, my mother and grandparents.

Find me somebody who doesn't clench up on the way into a funeral home, and you'll find a person who never lost someone they loved.

There was some consolation to suffering through this together, and we were all standing in our own little pack for support as we got to the red-carpeted steps. The door opened automatically, and we walked in to the oppressive quiet.

A suitably solemn Spring relative met us at the door, in a quiet gray suit (black would have suggested she was one of the mourners) and pointed us to the repose room where Mrs. Winch was running her last meeting.

As we walked down the hall, I allowed myself a small prayer of thanks this wasn't Western Pennsylvania. Back home, they laid 'em out and commented on how good they looked. Around here, closed casket is the standard, often just the cremation urn, and thank God for it.

Cremation urn.

It took everything I had not to go weak with relief when I saw it.

Mrs. Winch was indeed now reposing in an ugly olive ceramic urn, which seemed entirely appropriate. Which also meant she, and the poison that killed her, were dust.

We were absolutely in the clear on the death.

Madge and I still had to find the person who made the poison, and I had to get the Book back from Kryssie, but we might just get through this. We really might.

"I forgot to tell Madge something," I whispered to Corinna. "I don't want to be rude, but I have to text her."

She shrugged. "No big deal."

I turned aside and quickly texted Madge one word:

Cremated.

She would be as relieved as I was, and it wasn't fair to make her wait until I got home from this hot mess.

And hot mess it was.

Alcott doesn't really have enough people for a full-on mob scene, but it's fair to say it sure seemed like the whole town was crammed into Spring's. I didn't need to worry about anyone thinking I was rude for texting– I could have live-blogged it, and nobody would have noticed.

As the three of us reached the door of the repose room, I had a deeply inappropriate flash of the royals walking into Westminster Hall to pay tribute to the late queen. I wondered which ones we were.

Corinna and I *were* looking awfully sharp in dark slacks and blazers, hers cognac, mine violet. Not to mention Brian, who'd put a classic navy blazer over the chambray shirt and khakis he usually wore to mind the store.

Focus.

Alcott, like the rest of the world, has seen a pretty significant decline in dress and demeanor in recent years, and it was more than evident in the crowd. The only people in anything qualifying as formal wear were the widower, Ginny Pescatore, and a few other strays, probably Hartford or New Haven professionals who'd come from work. Everyone else was in variants of "athleisure," from almost elegant sweater-and-skinny pants combinations to cargo shorts.

Cargo shorts were the first thing we saw on the way in, on Burl Brewer, combined with a bright orange polo with a logo suggesting it was merch from a political rally. The hard-rightie councilman was buttonholing Morton Winch, apparently exercised in mind over cremation, which seemed both insensitive and a little late.

Ginny had set up what looked like her own separate power base on the other side of the room, sitting in a chair with George Germain and a couple of other council members surrounding her. It seemed a little off to me, her sitting there as if she were one of the bereaved, but maybe it was some sort of succession thing.

Ugh, the royals again.

Double ugh, Morton Winch.

I'd seen him around the library here and there and never been especially impressed. Or repulsed. Or anything.

The nebbish husband of the big mean wife is such a stereotype it's not even worth discussing anymore. Morton Winch wasn't quite that. He was just– disengaged.

Nothing much to look at, nothing much to say, nothing especially noticeable about him other than a fondness for old mysteries. One day when I was cataloging donations for the sale, he came in to see if we had any new ones.

He wasn't a Dick Francis guy like Al (and my grandfather), but a pulp guy. There's nothing wrong with those old tantalizing shoot 'em ups, but it speaks to the person that this very vanilla fella was into something so lurid.

Standing by the urn, Winch didn't look anguished as much as bored. As if paying appropriate tribute to his late wife was an inconvenience.

Considering his late wife, I supposed there was a case to be made for that.

"Ohh, Morty."

Funeral homes are a lot like libraries, only not fun, so the loud expression of sympathy split the air like a shot.

Everyone turned toward the urn to see the blonde woman from the zoning office draping herself on the widower in an extravagantly sympathetic embrace. Now that she wasn't behind a high counter, I could tell her sympathy wasn't the only thing extravagant about her. She was in a pink floral dress and cardigan, the sweater unbuttoned to offer a good view of the scoop neck of the dress, and the creamy skin beneath.

Quite a sight for a New England funeral.

Then, as she stroked Morton Winch's arm, something on her wrist caught the light. It was fairly far away, but distinctive.

It was indeed the Goldflower bracelet from the parking lot.

Morton Winch, who at least had some minimal sense of decorum, carefully detached himself from his friend and patted her hand. "I appreciate the sympathy, Sylvia."

"Of course."

He held her gaze. She backed up just a tiny bit as her face sharpened. Not scared of him. Making the same calculations he was. They were in on it together.

Whatever *it* was.

I couldn't really process then because it was almost our turn. Corinna and I were first, with Brian carefully hovering in the background. Michael does the same thing sometimes. I suppose it's a little sexist, but I find it sweet and reassuring from the standup guys in my life. Nice to have some backup.

"Oh, Corinna and Grace," Morton said, holding his hands out to us. His voice and bottom lip quivered a bit, but his eyes were dry.

As we shook hands, I noticed a scent.

I couldn't place it. Maybe it was just all those lilies and roses combined with a lightly spicy waft of expensive candles the Spring family had placed around the room. But there was something there.

"Thank you so much for trying to help poor Obie."

And just like that, any observations, or indeed any rational thoughts I might have had were drowned in a massive wave of inappropriate hilarity. If I looked at Corinna or Brian, I knew I would explode in giggles.

Beside me, Corinna was shaking.

Brian coughed, a snort-y noise that was almost certainly cover for a laugh too.

The three of us managed to shake hands and mumble something vaguely suitable to the moment and move on. Very quickly, but hopefully not indecently.

"Out." Corinna said it, but Brian and I were definitely moving the same way.

We actually did manage to get to the door and out into the parking lot before losing it.

Fortunately, we were far enough away from the next knot of people coming to pay respects that we didn't explode in their faces.

But honestly, it wouldn't have mattered.

"Obie." Corinna was the first one able to breathe again.

"Obie," I said.

"Of all the things I thought she was, an Obie was not one of them." Brian, blast him, obviously had much better breath control than the rest of us.

"Morty and Obie." I admit I said it just to start another round of howls. We'd earned it.

"There's so much bad there," Corinna took a breath and straightened herself out.

"And not in a good way." Brian shook his head. "Never saw that blonde coming."

I, of course, had a hint. But I didn't know how this was all going to fit together at the end, and I didn't want to give away anything I might need to use later. So I went with my other thought: "Morty must have something going on."

"Ick." Corinna's face twisted in disgust. "Seriously?"

"I knew straight people were weird, but *that* weird?" Brian wrinkled his nose. "And really just tacky."

"Yeah," I agreed. "Whatever your orientation, I don't think the side person is supposed to come to the wake."

"Morty and Obie may have had some kind of deal," Corinna said. "But that doesn't mean flaunting it."

"Exactly." I nodded.

"And speaking of flaunting it, did you see Ginny Pescatore practically holding a political action committee meeting in the corner?" Brian asked.

"That was pretty nuts," I agreed.

"She's been at this for a while," Corinna said. "One of my friends in New Haven says she's been meeting with the county party."

"Really?" I asked. "State house or something like that?"

"Maybe." Corinna took a breath and thought about it. "My friend seems to think she has her eye on the congressional seat. You know Lucy DiLuca's going to retire after the next election, and Ginny apparently has hopes."

"From town council vice-chair to Congress?" Brian gave a low whistle. "That's a lot even for Ginny."

"But if she's running the council," I said, thinking out loud, "and does some high-profile stuff to move the town in a different direction..."

"Say funding the library and pulling off the outlet mall deal?" Corinna nodded.

"Then she might have something to throw out there," Brian admitted. "Not quite as crazy as it sounds now."

Now that Obie (inappropriate snicker) Winch was dead.

So, make that one more person with a very good motive and possible access to the Book.

"Don't tell me you three already did your duty." Moira was just walking into the parking lot. She'd told Corinna she would come over when she could but wasn't sure when that would be.

"We did. Sorry," I said.

Moira sighed. "You would."

"Don't worry, I'm sure there's still plenty of the Morty and Obie show," Brian said.

"Obie?" Moira's eyes widened.

"Obie," Corinna confirmed.

"Mr. Winch thanked us for our efforts to help 'Obie,'" I said.

"Oh, dear Lord." Now Moira was trying to stop inappropriate giggles. "I hate you guys."

"Why should we have all the fun?" Corinna asked. "You'll be fine. And make sure to get a look at the girlfriend."

"Girlfriend?"

"She was with him at the urn when we were there," Brian told her.

"At the *urn*?" Something changed in Moira's face. She looked exactly the way I felt when I saw Mrs. Winch had been cremated.

I knew why I'd felt that way. And I had a terrible feeling I knew why she did too.

Prosecutors call it consciousness of guilt. People often give themselves away because they know they're guilty long before anyone else does.

In my other profession, we're taught to avoid any hint of it. Just because we know we've made something happen doesn't mean anyone else does. If you act innocent, people will assume you are.

Vice versa too.

Moira recovered quickly, and I doubted Corinna or Brian even caught it. The only reason I did was my background.

"Well, then," Moira said.

"Yep." I kept my tone normal. I certainly didn't need to give anything away.

"That's not all," Corinna continued. "Ginny Pescatore is practically holding a meeting on the other side of the wake."

"Seriously?"

"Seriously," I confirmed.

"Apparently lining up her political ducks," Brian added, with a nod to Corinna.

"Friend of mine in New Haven says Ginny's been eyeing Lucy DiLuca's congressional seat."

Moira shook her head. "And you're throwing me into all of this alone?"

We all squirmed a little. Moira could do librarian voice better than anyone when she wanted to.

Then she laughed. To me, it sounded relieved, the kind of laugh you give when you haven't been able to relax for a while. But I could have been picking up stuff that wasn't there. "I'll manage. Might actually be fun."

"Not for Morty," Brian said.

Corinna and I weren't trying for unison, but the next two words did indeed come out in chorus: "Or Obie."

CHAPTER 25
HOME FRONT BLUES

B ack at the hardware store, Old Man Loquat was regaling a rapt audience with a carefully edited WWII story. No surprise the three little ones were interested, but he'd actually gotten Imani to put down her tablet and listen. Major achievement.

"...and that's why it's really important to remember people are people, kids. Because once we start thinking folks are bad just because of who they are, it doesn't take long to start putting up the barbed wire."

I knew, because Brian had told me, Mr. Loquat was on a squad that liberated one of the camps. He never said a lot about it, but every once in a while, he would make a small, but pointed reference. And if kids asked him about the war, he'd tell them enough to make it clear.

He saw the three of us coming and sent us an impish grin. "But you know, kids, while we did a lot of important stuff, we had some fun together too. Did I ever tell you about the time we had to get through a field of sheep to the next town? My buddy from the Bronx had never seen a live sheep and..."

Brian, Corinna, and I exchanged glances and waited for the rest of the story along with the kids. It was a doozy, involving the sheep, three soldiers, and a passing Nazi patrol. Let's just say everyone who deserved to get covered in sheep manure did, and Old Man Loquat and his buddies got a good dinner at the sheep-herder's house.

Happily grossed out, the kids scattered to their respective parents, and Mr. Loquat accepted thanks.

"Always glad to spend time with the little ones. They keep you young," he observed. Jimmy Stewart yowled from her shelf. Obviously, she had a far lower opinion of juvenile humans than her keeper. I didn't doubt she'd climbed right up to her spot the minute the kids arrived.

"Oh, fine, Jim. Be that way." The old man took his cat down and cradled her, earning the purr.

Daniel and Cherise watched, clearly wanting to pet her, but the glint in Jimmy's gold eyes made it very clear she had exactly zero interest in their attention.

Imani favored her mother with a hello that just barely scraped over the standard for minimum politeness and whipped out her tablet.

The grownups made quick goodbyes, and Corinna headed for her car in the library lot. The last I heard of her was "How many times do I have to tell you not to walk with that thing?"

Coming attractions, I had to assume.

I wasn't sure I was ready for that movie.

Still, if Corinna could handle it…

"Ma! I'm hungry." Daniel pulled on my arm.

Oh. Dinner.

Surely there was something in the freezer. Burgers, maybe. Chicken cutlets for the thrown-together chicken parmigiana that would scandalize the Italian *nonnas* of New Haven County, but made a fast and easy worknight meal.

"How do you feel about chicken parm?" I asked.

"Yum!"

Well, that's one less thing to worry about.

It should have been, anyhow, until Ward Cleaver walked in

the door about five minutes after we did. Michael put down his brief bag and greeted Daniel with a big hug, then walked into the kitchen with a look of anticipation I knew a little too well.

"What? Dinner's not ready yet?" Maybe more like Archie Bunker.

"No," I said, doing my best to manage a friendly tone. "We were at the calling hours for Mrs. Winch, remember?"

"You took Daniel to the calling hours?"

"Of course not," I replied, still managing cool and sweet despite my own more than stressful day. I knew this one. Michael wasn't really a sexist jerk. He was tired and hungry and wound too tightly about the corruption case.

I could give him a little rope. Not a lot, just a little.

"Daniel– and Cherise, Imani, and Zoey– got a fun hour of war stories with Old Man Loquat."

"Could do worse." Michael nodded, taking the chance to back off. "I'd go for that."

"Definitely better than a deeply weird wake."

"Weird how?"

"Well, Morton Winch's girlfriend came up to comfort him at the urn."

"At the urn?" Michael asked, his eyes widening.

"At the actual urn." The pasta water was boiling, so I took the box of linguine out of the cabinet.

"Good turnout?"

"I think everyone in town was there. Probably everybody but your client."

"Not funny." Michael scowled. "He's into town affairs up to his eyeballs. And his firm is, in fact, involved in the new outlet mall proposal."

"Sorry." I took a big handful of linguine, broke it in half, and dropped it in the hot water. The *nonnas* probably wouldn't be okay with that either, but when you're feeding a six-year-old, compromises must be made.

"What's for dinner?"

"Chicken parm," I said. "Fast and tasty, and Daniel loves it."

Michael winced.

"What?"

"Had a chicken parm sub at DiLuca's for lunch."

"And I'm supposed to know that how?"

"Well, if you put a little effort into planning meals instead of just throwing chicken parm together at the end of the day -"

"Excuse me?" And that, for those of you who haven't been married for a dozen years, is how to get an ugly stupid fight started. "Do you think I sit around all day doing nothing?"

"Of course not," he said, his tone weary and exasperated. "But I do think you could at least come up with a plan when you know you're going to have a busy day."

"I've got a plan for you, pal." I stirred the pasta.

"Ma! Scotchie's getting into the paint again!"

Saved by the kid and dog. At least for the moment.

"I've got it, buddy." Michael called. "Why don't we go out in the yard and throw the tennis ball around while Mom finishes dinner?"

"Great, Dad!"

I reminded myself as I assembled the meal that my son needs a father so cracking Michael's skull with the pasta pot was not an option. If only because I wouldn't have him to defend me. Not that a jury with one married woman on it would have convicted me.

It would have blown over if Michael hadn't looked at his (actually quite appetizing) plate of pasta and chicken with a nice coating of good jarred sauce and perfectly melted mozz and sighed. I knew what that meant, and I wasn't accepting delivery.

Dinner conversation, what there was of it, centered on Daniel and school. When I'm really annoyed with Michael, I don't talk to him except for matters related to our son. Yes, it's pretty passive-aggressive, but it's better than having my son hear me call his father every name in the book.

Michael, being Michael, didn't even figure out how angry I

was until dinner was over, and I was cleaning up. He brought the plates into the kitchen and rinsed them, which was one step better than he usually managed on a day like this, and looked at me.

"Did I do something?"

I took a breath. I could have emptied the jar of sauce in my hand over his head, but then I'd have to send his shirt to the cleaner's and wash the floor. "I don't know, Ward, did you?"

"Are you mad because I had chicken parm for lunch?"

"No, I'm mad because you were a jerk about it." I put the sauce jar in the fridge and picked up the pasta pot. "I may not get a big retainer for my work, but it is work."

"I know that. You're raising my son. It's a huge job."

"*Your* son?"

"Our son." Michael sighed. "Look, I'm tired and stressed, and I don't need to parse every little word for appropriate feminist validation tonight."

"Fine."

"Tweety-"

"I'm sure you have important work to do," I said, in a cold steely tone. "I have to finish cleaning up the kitchen, make sure *your* son does his homework, and then perhaps spend a little time on those documents you asked me to look at. If you don't think my brain has atrophied from a steady diet of chicken parm."

"C'mon. I'm not-"

"Oh, you are."

"Fine." Michael gave me that dismissive shrug he does so well. "I have work to do. Maybe you'll cool off in an hour or so."

"Don't count on it."

We did a very good job of playing nice while putting Daniel to bed, as we always do when we're having one of these arguments, and then returned to our corners. I was just mad enough at Michael that I simply made sure the documents we had matched his discovery list and left it there before returning to my own work. Paid and professional work, thank you very much.

Nineteenth-century poisoners sounded like a lot of fun right about now.

The proposal still wasn't my idea of a great read by the time I knocked off a couple hours later, but it finally looked like something, and the writing had some decent flow to it.

The really good news was my client was cool. She emailed me earlier in the day, though I hadn't gotten to it until now, saying she trusted my judgment, and she was more interested in having an accurate and readable proposal than keeping her own lovely words.

I wondered if she'd be willing to train Michael on how to handle criticism.

Not fair, I knew. Michael, like me, was always willing to accept changes to make his work better. He was a true pro and a good colleague.

Just sometimes a real jerk at home.

By the time I saved the almost-final draft of the proposal, Michael had gone to bed and turned on some goofy comedy from the streaming service. We are not one of those couples who obsess about not going to bed angry.

In fact, sometimes sleeping it off helps us.

A little distance, and a little rest, can dull the sharp edges, and we usually wake up in the wee hours unable to remember why we were so angry. Not that we don't know what the issues are– those never really change– but with some time, they matter less than being together.

If I had to guess, I'd say this simple calculation is the reason Michael and I always work it out. My theory, and since I've managed to stay married for a dozen years I think there's something to it, is that maintaining a marriage is a skill like any other. You develop strategies and reflexes, just like you do when you're doing anything else that matters to you.

All in the service of a pretty simple idea: the marriage is more important than winning any given argument.

Keeping that in mind does go a long way in defusing things.

Even if I want to drop an anvil on his stupid clueless head sometimes.

He was snoring when I climbed into bed.

That wasn't a surprise.

It was a surprise he didn't wake up in the night.

I did at about three, and lay there for an hour or so listening to him breathe and feeling surprisingly bereft.

It wasn't just the fight.

Things felt very ugly and uncertain here. I didn't know how all of this was going to end, and I didn't want to leave it like this with Michael.

If...

Failure, said Professor Munroe, was not an option.

Nope.

I turned over and curled up into a ball and waited for exhaustion to drag me back into sleep. It took an awful lot longer than I hoped it would.

CHAPTER 26
BRIGHT AND SURLY

Friday morning dawned cold. Seriously cold.

The kind of cold that reminds us Connecticut residents we really do live in New England, and winter really is on the way.

At least the chill didn't last long between Michael and me.

He straggled into the kitchen, as the coffeemaker beeped, with a sad little boy look that would not have been out of place on Daniel.

Or Scotchie.

He took a mug out of the cabinet and walked over to me. "Please, may I have a drop?"

I tried for a hard look but couldn't quite stop the smile. "I suppose."

"I know you'd like to put arsenic in it..."

"Nah," I said, pouring. "Arsenic is too slow and too easily detectable."

"That's right. You're working on that book proposal on the old Coulter case."

"Yep." Not that he'd ever suspect my real reason for expertise with poison. "It's finally coming together pretty well too."

"Can't say the same for my case." He bent into the mug and

took a deep breath. It was too hot to drink, but apparently the fumes were enough. "Still hate me?"

"I never hated you." I didn't stop the crisp, slightly irritated, note in my voice.

"Well, that's a start." He set the mug down and put his hands on my shoulders. "Look. I was probably a first-rate sexist pig jerk yesterday."

"Impressive sexist pig jerk." I smiled a little.

"And all true." He pushed back a stray strand of my hair, and his thumb lingered on my cheekbone. "I'm not great at appreciating you when I'm drowning. I will try to do better."

"That's a nice start." Better than that. There's probably some woman somewhere who could brush off a basically good guy admitting he blew it, but I'm not her.

"Thank you. How about I bring home a pizza from Pepe's tonight, and we open a nice bottle of wine later?"

"Sorry, babe," I said. "We have plans."

"We do?"

"PTA ice cream social."

"Do we have to?"

"We do." I wrapped my arms around his neck. "But that doesn't mean we can't kiss and make up later."

"Kiss now. Make up later." Michael pulled me in.

If he were just a little less hot, or a little less sincere in his apologies, I might reconsider that arsenic. Or something else. But he's Michael.

"ICK!"

Daniel– and Scotchie– were in the kitchen doorway.

"Someday, Daniel Bruce," Michael said, "you will have a wonderful partner, and you will want to keep them happy with you."

"Breakfast would make me happy," Daniel assured him. "Don't need kissy stuff."

I sighed. "French toast sticks then."

"Yes, please."

"C'mon, Scotchie. Let's go for a run." Michael planted a kiss on my cheek. "Got a motion hearing today, and I need to burn off a little static."

"Put on a fleece. The digital thingie says it's 32 degrees."

"It has a name," Michael said.

"Yes, and if you say it, the thingie will wake up and ask us what we want. That is precisely what we do *not* want."

"Fair enough." He turned back as he headed for the door. "We're good?"

We would have been if he hadn't asked for affirmation everything was all right. I couldn't quite get there, considering how often this happened. "As good as we need to be."

"Meaning I need to do better," Michael said.

"Oh, yeah. Getting kind of bored with this one."

"Duly noted." Michael held my gaze. "I do get it, you know, Tweety."

He doesn't. But he does try, and that's worth a lot.

"We're fine, Michael." I walked over and kissed his cheek. "Been a tough week. Let's just get through the day and have a nice evening."

"I vote for that too."

Scotchie woofed.

"I'm hungry, Ma!"

"Daniel," Michael said, as he headed for Scotchie, "your mother works very hard. She'll have your breakfast in a minute."

"Sorry, Dad."

Michael ruffled his hair. "Respect's always a good thing, pal."

"Okay."

Hard to stay mad at a guy who's actually trying to raise your son to respect you and all women. Wretch.

Scotchie scratched at the door as Michael grabbed the fleece he kept on a hook for just these occasions.

That reminded me.

I'd better make sure Daniel and I were ready for drop-off while I was thinking of it.

After I put the French toast sticks in the microwave, I dug Daniel's lined windbreaker out of the hall closet and reached for my own barn jacket. The navy twill jacket felt heavy when I pulled it out. Not heavy like the first time you pick up a cold-weather garment in months.

Heavy like there was something in the pockets.

That's when I remembered I hadn't worn it since I'd gone for a walk with Scotchie after the book fair. I'd been cold from the stress of everything that happened.

And I'd put the pockets to good use at the scene.

Maybe I had something that would give me a direction now.

In one pocket I found the ugly brown-and-orange scarf in the pooper-scooper bag where I'd stuffed it, what seemed like a year ago. Thanks to the bag, it still smelled of some awful cologne that now seemed vaguely familiar. With the fainter, but still detectable (at least to my trained nose) scent of subtle poison.

If I could just remember where I'd smelled that disgusting cologne.

The reek, thanks to the bag, was still pretty impressive. I re-tied the bag and tossed it in the corner of the closet. It probably wasn't dangerous, just repulsive, but I wasn't taking any chances. Nobody would look in the bottom of the closet, and I could ditch it later.

At least, since the horrible thing had been bagged, my jacket didn't smell like a 1970's singles bar.

Some minor consolation.

About all the consolation I got that morning considering what I found in the other pocket: the most damning piece of evidence yet.

It seemed innocent enough, just a small plastic container, circular with a red top. But I opened it and knew immediately. Not somebody's leftover salad dressing. Our poison.

Someone had actually made a batch of subtle poison.

And unfortunately, now I was pretty sure who.

As I'd seen when Cherise dropped her lunch the other day,

Corinna's plastic containers were a fancy set with blue lids. This wasn't one of the disposable ones, but a step up. And it was a little bit discolored from earlier use.

Worse, I remembered seeing an almost identical one on Moira's desk two days before.

Confirmation of the last thing I wanted to believe.

My friend had done it. And now, I was going to have to deal with it.

Probably deal with her.

I needed to think about this.

The best thing I could do was take care of getting the Book back and confront Moira when I got a chance.

Maybe tonight. I knew she'd be at the social recruiting for the Friends of the Library.

She needed a whole different kind of friends now.

And there was no way I could let this wait until tonight. None.

She was often at the library early before it opened. I could go over after drop-off and settle this.

Settle it how?

I didn't want to think about that just yet. Nor did I want to think about bringing in Madge or Professor Munroe. Not until I absolutely had to go there.

Maybe there was still a way out. Maybe I could talk to Moira, find out what happened, and come up with some kind of plan based on that.

Professor Munroe had told me to resolve matters without unnecessary action after all.

The microwave beeped.

"Is that my breakfast?" Daniel asked.

I was still holding the container. I shoved it in the pocket of the barn jacket and tossed the jacket on a kitchen chair out of the way. The poison was at least six days old and had probably lost most of its potency. But it had been in a container all that time, and I didn't know how that would affect things.

Better to take no chances.

Fortunately, Daniel didn't ask why I washed my hands twice before I touched his plate.

Drop-off was pretty routine. Well, except for that container burning a hole in the pocket of my jacket.

Corinna and Brian looked as tired as I felt.

We all mumbled promises to meet at the social and waved the kids off to their day.

It had been a hard week for everyone.

Some harder than others...and it wasn't getting easier from here.

When I got back to the car though, I got at least a little joy, an email from Al. I'd sent him pics of five different rings, all bands of various designs, from simple stones to wreaths of flowers.

THIS ONE, he'd captioned a pic of a really lovely ruby-and-gold band with an intricate beaded design.

Absolutely perfect! All good wishes! I replied.

Now it was up to me to make sure they had a chance to get their happy ending.

First, the library.

Moira's car was in the lot alone.

Good. We'd want to do this in private.

The door was locked, but Moira was in the lobby, and she let me right in.

"Hey, Grace, what's up?"

"Got a minute?" I asked, as neutrally as I could.

"Sure. Come over here."

We walked over to the desk in the center of the circulation area. She had an office in the back of the building, but this one, out in the open, was her usual spot. I've never seen anyone else using it, and it was covered with the ordinary stuff of a normal day. Some books, mail, a padded lunchbox. A cup of coffee.

She watched me while we sat. Moira's no fool. She knew something was coming here.

Might as well just do it.

In it to win it.

I took a breath. I hated this. It's one thing to take out predators who've spent most of their time on this earth destroying innocent lives. It's another thing entirely to ask a good friend if she's done murder.

Yeah, I know. Irony alert.

Finally, I just did the obvious thing. I took the plastic container out of my jacket pocket and put it on the desk.

The blood drained from Moira's face, and her eyes widened. For one horrible instant, I thought she stopped breathing. "What..."

"I could ask you the same."

"What do you..." she started.

"I know enough. I know you made this from the recipe in the Book. What I can't figure out is why...or how you thought you'd get away with it."

A sigh. "I didn't, really. I've spent the last week expecting the cops to come after me."

"They won't," I said. "The death case is closed."

"I know that after last night. But there's still someone who had the book with the untraceable poison recipe. I'm worried what they might do."

"That's not an unreasonable concern."

"Do you think they'll come after me?"

"Well, they are. In a manner of speaking."

She met my gaze. A little frightened, a lot disappointed. "What does that mean?"

"I'm not sure yet," I admitted. "The less you know, the better chance we have to get out of this."

"We do?"

"Maybe. Tell me what happened."

Moira took a deep breath. When she spoke, her voice was wobbly. "She wanted to cut the budget in half. I would have had to fire Corinna, and even then..."

I put my hand on her arm, and she met my gaze, her eyes a little damp.

"I need this job."

"I know. So you saw a recipe for untraceable poison, and you thought you'd try it?"

"Made sense at the time. I was looking at the book while I was cataloging things, and the recipe was right there on the flyleaf. Winch had been all over me just a few minutes before, and I thought 'Hey, why not?' It was all stuff I had around the house or could buy at the Super Duper. And what if it actually worked? What if I could really take her out and save the library. And Mom, of course."

"Right."

"Mom's Medicare doesn't cover the full cost of the home. If I lose my job, she's going to have to go somewhere that accepts what Medicare and Medicaid will pay. I'm not ashamed to admit I would have killed to spare her from one of those places."

I knew plenty of sandwich-generation folks who'd do the same. My grandmother had spent her last years with dementia in the only home my mother could afford. I remembered the smell. Care *had* to be better now, but still. I nodded. "Anyone who's been there would understand."

"They would." Another ragged breath, and a bitter little laugh. "But I couldn't do it."

"What?" My turn to stare.

"I brought it. I was going to put it on the financial report she'd demanded...nice piece of irony, right?"

"Right." I wasn't really sure it would have worked. We don't usually transfer it from objects.

"But I couldn't do it." She shook her head. "I was the only one on the desk, so it was safe enough. I had the report and the container on my desk with the recipe open...and there was some kind of circulation crisis. I don't even remember what."

"Okay." That much made sense. I've been there when someone decides they need an inter-library loan of books on crochet in Victorian Britain, or the book club wants to reserve eighteen copies of the new erotic thriller. Moira can get drawn away for a long time.

"And while I was dealing with that, I realized I'm not a killer. Just not the kind of person who could really do that. I'm not sure what sort of sickness, or moral flaw, somebody needs to do it, but I don't have it."

"Yeah?" I asked, keeping my voice as neutral as possible. It would not help to point out sometimes it isn't a moral flaw, but a mission from an Archangel.

"Yeah. Just knew I couldn't live with it if I did."

Better to keep silent. Anything I said could have been incriminating, or insulting, or just plain wrong in so many ways. She continued speaking.

"Oh, you wouldn't understand. You'd never think about killing someone just to save your job."

"Moira," I said quietly, "you'd be surprised what someone might be capable of doing if they had to."

She held my gaze for a long moment.

"Oh."

"Why don't you tell me what happened next."

"Well, when I turned back to the desk, the container was gone. The Book was still there and the financial report, but not the container."

"Gone?"

"Gone."

"So someone just grabbed it off your desk– while it was sitting there next to the recipe?"

"That's what happened. I know how it sounds, but it's really what happened."

I raised a hand to my forehead, trying to massage away the start of yet another headache. "This is actively nuts."

"I'm aware of that." She sighed. "I was terrified. I closed the book and ransacked my desk, but the thing was gone. Somebody took it. And since I'd been dumb enough to leave the book open..."

"They knew exactly what it was and how to use it."

"Yep."

"Do you know who was in the library that day?"

"Well, after all that, I looked around. I couldn't just run up to folks asking if they'd stolen my poison, you know."

"Probably not."

"But Ginny was there, and Al, and George Germain. And Morton Winch too. I mean, it could have been anyone."

"And that's where you left it?"

She glared at me. "What was I going to do? Announce on the PA 'the Circulation Desk is missing some undetectable poison'?"

"Probably not. Didn't you suspect something when she dropped dead?"

"I didn't suspect. I was pretty sure." A tear oozed out of one eye, and she dashed it away. "It was too much of a coincidence."

"And..."

"And I wasn't going to go to the cops and tell them I made the poison." She took a breath. "But it's still my fault. I'm an accessory."

"Not in any legal sense," I assured her, even if the law was the last thing she needed to worry about. "If someone takes something out of your possession– and having it on your desk means it is in your possession– then uses it for evil purpose, it is not your fault. If you actively give them the poison knowing they will probably use it to kill, that's different."

"That's not what I did."

"No."

"So I'm not legally liable for it?"

"First of all," I reminded her, "as far as the law is concerned, Mrs. Winch died of natural causes, and since she's been cremated, there is no way to prove otherwise."

Moira nodded. "Okay."

"So there's not going to be any legal liability. You can stop worrying about that."

"That helps."

"Good." I gave her an encouraging smile. "But as far as the ethics of the thing go, you didn't deliberately walk away from the desk with the idea that someone would pick up the poison and use it, so you're also clear there."

Another nod. A deep breath. "This is really over then?"

"It's on its way to being over, at least for you."

"What does that mean?"

I took a breath, still processing and trying to figure out where to go from here.

She pointed to the container. "Why do you have it?"

"I found it in the trash at the library after the fair."

Moira nodded, studied me. We've been friends for a while, and she knew me well enough to know there was more. The next question wasn't really a surprise:

"How are you in this?"

Long pause. I thought about it. She knew about the Book, but she wasn't going to run out and tell the world. And she didn't know anything else. Not about the sisterhood or what we did with that Book. No guilty knowledge to eliminate.

There really might be a safe way forward for her.

I still had to figure out who got the poison and used it...but I might at least be able to keep Moira out of this.

That's a win.

"I can't tell you that," I said. "If I do, you'll be in a lot bigger trouble than you are now."

She just *looked* at me for a moment. Assessing me. Absorbing the realization the friend she'd always considered a normal decent person like her could actually be someone else entirely. "Okay."

"Here's what we're going to do," I said. "I'm going to figure out the rest of this."

"What am I going to do?"

"Absolutely nothing. You're going to go on from here as if we never had this conversation."

"Grace, you don't have to…"

"Moira."

"Oh."

"Yeah." I took a breath. "The best thing you can do is forget you ever saw the Book. And definitely everything after that."

"Are you speaking as a lawyer?" she asked.

"That'll do." I chose my next words with care. "I am speaking as a friend who has your best interests and safety at heart.

"Safety?"

"Safety."

She looked from me to the container and back again. I didn't know how much was getting through, but it was enough. A breath. A nod. "How will I know everything is okay?"

"For you, everything is okay as of now. As long as you don't tell anyone about the Book or the poison, you have nothing to worry about."

"Never?"

"Never." I held her gaze. "So go on from here."

"I'm safe?"

"You're safe. As long as you never speak of this again to me or anyone. Anyone."

"I'm not in the habit of running around confessing things." She patted my hand. "Thank you, Grace."

I managed a smile. "Don't thank me yet."

"What-"

I just looked at her.

"Right." She nodded. "Can I wish you luck?"

"Sure. I'm going to need it."

CHAPTER 27
IF IT'S NOT ONE THING...

B ack in the car, I tried to think it through.

The good news is Moira was safe.

She wasn't a gossipy person anyhow, and she clearly knew she was potentially in at least as much trouble as I was, even if she didn't know everything in play. So I wouldn't have to worry about her.

The problem was whoever picked up that poison.

They probably weren't much of a threat to the sisterhood, honestly, since anyone who took the poison and left the Book wouldn't have much in the way of useful, read dangerous, knowledge.

And they'd attribute anything they did know to Moira, not Madge or me, so as long as I got the Book back from Kryssie, we were in the clear. Mission accomplished, and sisterhood protected without any unnecessary taking of life.

Professor Munroe would be pleased.

Except there was still someone out there who had killed a person with our poison. A person who did not deserve it, however much she might have deserved other unpleasantness.

Professor Munroe might, or might not, care about that.

But I certainly did.

Which meant, despite everything else, I still had a killer to catch.

Who?

Good question.

Well, one mess at a time. Get the Book back tonight, destroy it, and then worry about the cleanup. Madge and Professor Munroe might have some thoughts on how to handle that, and I could seek their counsel later.

Once the Book was in our hands.

The end, I thought, might just be in sight.

Or at least the worst might be over.

Sometimes my naïveté amuses even me.

Back home, I decided the best thing I could do was get some work done.

I returned to the documents, trying to figure out what I was missing. I know prosecutors like to throw everything at a big case, but it wasn't adding up. It looked to me like they were trying to get away with something no reasonable judge would allow.

Didn't make sense at all.

But maybe I had missed something because I'd been upset about Moira. Even though I'm very good at compartmentalizing, that had been a pretty tough lift.

Coffee. Everything's better with caffeine.

While the coffee brewed, I decided to switch projects for a bit and let whatever was bothering me about the documents work its way to the surface naturally.

I was up to the copy edit on the book proposal. Perfect. Copy editing uses a different part of the brain, and the heavy logical reasoning part of my mind might just relax enough to free some thoughts on the documents.

Fresh cup in hand, I was just opening the book proposal file when the phone rang.

Michael's office.

"Grace, we have a problem." Annie, his paralegal, sounded

upset and scared, entirely different from her usual relaxed demeanor.

"What?"

"Michael's been held in contempt."

I let out the breath I'd been holding. Annie's tone had really scared me. I knew enough about the world to know I could survive without Michael...and also to know I didn't want to. "Okay. What happened?"

"It's the corruption case. He got into it with Judge Burdette over something the prosecutors want to introduce. Not a hundred percent sure what. I think it was in the stuff you've got– the prior bad acts evidence they're trying to get in."

I was willing to bet I knew. He'd seen the same thing I had. But why get heated– and why challenge Judge Veronica Burns Burdette, the most formidable jurist on the New Haven bench? Not a good call.

The stress of the case was getting to him.

And it probably didn't help we'd had a stupid fight last night. It's never just one thing. It's everything.

Michael doesn't have a temper– until he does. I've only seen him really angry a few times and never in public. But with a case that was a stretch, and some questionable behavior from the prosecution...maybe.

"Where is he now?"

"Holding in a client room. Judge says she'll send him to the lockup if he doesn't apologize by the end of the day."

I sighed. A contest of wills was not going to go well. Michael was not known for giving ground– and it was entirely possible Judge Burdette had never been wrong in her threescore and ten on this earth.

"He needs a lawyer, Grace, and more, he needs somebody to talk a little sense into him."

"That he does," I agreed.

"So you'll come?"

"Of course. Give me an hour to put on my court suit and drive down there."

"An hour's good. He might cool off."

"Oh, he won't." I didn't need to encourage false hope. "But it might give him enough time to think about what a fine mess he's gotten himself into."

I hit end and checked the time. 11:45.

Fortunately, it was the day Brian had some help at the store. He could pick up Daniel along with Zoey. I dialed as I walked into the bedroom and rummaged in the back of my closet.

"Hey," I said. "Got a little situation…"

"What's up? I've got some intel."

"Yeah? Can it wait a minute?"

"Sure."

"Michael just got himself held in contempt. I have to go down there and straighten things out…can you pick up Daniel?"

"Absolutely. Contempt? Michael?"

"Something extra is going on here. I just don't know what."

Brian chuckled. "There's a lot of extra going around."

"Oh?" My last court suit was in the back of the closet, but it still looked good. Lightweight black wool twill, well and simply cut, it was the one I wore for opening and closing arguments when I was prosecuting.

"Yeah. Guess who I saw getting up to something at town hall this morning?"

"George Germain?"

"Uh, please. I'm going to have to go put out my mind's eye on that one."

I laughed. "He likes you."

"He likes acting like an ally. Big difference."

"Oh, I know," I said, as I flipped through hangers. The white oxford I used to wear with the court suit was long gone, but I had a purple t-shirt sweater that would do. "So who is it?"

"Morton Winch."

"The new-made widower?"

"None other," Brian said.

I bent down to the bottom of the closet where layers of old shoes and assorted debris had accumulated. Hopefully, my sensible heels were in there somewhere.

"With that woman from the calling hours?"

"Yep. And not just any woman, thanks. I only found out today when I went to see about getting a permit for the porch rebuild. She's a zoning officer."

"Zoning officer," I said. I'd thought she was an assistant when I saw her at town hall, but with the budget cuts everyone was probably doing extra work. Didn't that make life interesting. "And how do you know she's not just a friend?"

"Well, she got out of his car and leaned in and gave him a kiss on her way in."

"You saw?"

"I couldn't *not* see. You know how they don't open the offices until the precise second it turns over 9am? He pulled up at 8:58, let her out, and she turned back and gave him a big kiss."

"Well, then." As soon as I got off the line with him, I had to dive into the closet to find those pumps. "Already taking the girlfriend to work."

"Probably stayed over last night to console him." Brian sighed. "I don't want to be mean. I really don't. When I – when Jamie…I might have thought about it."

He had a hard time even saying his late husband's name. I wished we were in person so I could give him a hug. "Honey, this was not that, and you are not being unkind."

"I know," he said. "And maybe that bothers me most of all."

"Yeah. Got to be upsetting to know someone put so little value on their partner after what you've been through."

"Exactly. Just rotten." Brian took a deep breath and when he spoke again, his voice was almost back to normal. "Anyhow, I'll be happy to collect Daniel, and he can help Zoey drive my great-uncle crazy until you get Michael out of jail."

"He's not in jail…yet."

"Your job to keep him out then." He managed a laugh. "Good luck."

"I'm afraid I'm going to need it."

Brian cut off the call, and I returned to rummaging out a court outfit.

Ten minutes later, I was in the suit– thrilled it still fit– with a little light appropriate makeup on, and the coffee poured into a travel mug. I made sure my bar card and my admittedly outdated courthouse ID were still in my wallet (they were, which I suppose is telling) and dropped it in my bag. The big purple leather tote wasn't designed as a brief bag, but I'd tossed my worn one years ago.

It would do, though I hoped no Legos would fall out in the middle of arguments.

By then, I'd had a little time to think, taken one more look at the document list, and confirmed what I suspected. If Michael had seen the same thing, he might well have been furious at what the prosecution was trying to do– and reacted accordingly.

There was definitely an argument to be made, but I doubted Michael would calm down enough to make it.

I suspected the law, and the facts, weren't going to be the problem this time.

Nope. That would be my brand-new client.

CHAPTER 28
BOYS WILL BE...

Michael stood when I walked into the counsel room.

He looked a little rumpled, and the lean look his face always had during a big case had sharpened into something more.

"Hey." I nodded to the bailiff, an older African-American woman who was familiar. "Thanks, Edwards."

"Well, how about you? About time you came back from the mommy break."

I shrugged. "Family stuff, you know."

"Yep. Took a job up in Winsted for a while because I could get my daughter into a better high school. Happier here."

"Nothing like it."

We shared a smile.

"You know this one ticked off Judge Burdette?"

"I do." I sighed. "Let's see what I can do."

I turned to Michael.

"Counselor," he said. His hand moved toward me, and then back, as he realized it was very inappropriate to reach for his lawyer the way he did his wife.

"So?" I asked.

186

"Well, I was making a rather emphatic point with Judge Burdette and-"

Edwards cleared her throat. It *might* have been the court-house dust.

"Probably too emphatic. I should have calibrated better." Michael had that bad little boy face again, looking like Daniel trying to scam another cookie.

If only it were so simple.

"All right." I sat down at the table, well aware Michael was taking a good, appreciative look at my court suit. I'd be lying if I tried to tell you I didn't enjoy it. "Did they send you to the holding area?"

"Yep." A rueful sigh. "I could have clients for the rest of my life."

"Want to stay?"

"No, thanks."

My own rueful sigh. "It is my considered legal advice that you should throw yourself on the mercy of the court and promise never to behave in such a fashion again."

Michael squirmed.

I held his gaze.

"I agree."

"Good."

"But she-" His ears were pink, and I knew that expression.

"My professional advice, Counselor," I began, giving him the wifely look of death, "is to rage in the car on the way home."

"She's going to let them bring up-"

"I have heard of a little thing called the appeal process."

"I know, but this shouldn't even be a matter of argument." He ran a hand through his hair. "It really shouldn't."

"Correct me if I've missed anything here. It's Judge Burdette's courtroom. She believes it's a matter of argument."

"Yes."

"I seem to remember a certain federal law clerk telling me

187

when I lost a ruling on evidence that it's better to smile and appeal than to draw a contempt charge."

Michael shook his head. "I hate when you're right."

I shrugged.

Edwards nodded to us. "Judge is ready."

"So are we."

I led the way into the courtroom with Michael following, managing a docile face even as he muttered under his breath.

"I hate this."

"You'll live to fight another day."

"I can't stand seeing my client get railroaded and that SOB Winch-"

"Winch?" There couldn't be two people with shady dealings named Winch. Not even here.

"Unindicted co-conspirator-"

"ALL RISE!" Edwards called. "New Haven County Superior Court is in session. The Honorable Veronica Braden Burdette presiding."

Judge Burdette, an impossibly tiny white-haired woman with eyes that flashed blue fire, turned her imposing gaze on Michael and held it long enough to make him wilt a little.

It was part of the deal, and they both knew it.

Then she turned to me. And smiled. "Ah, and who do we have of counsel for Mr. Adair?"

"Grace MacInnes Adair, Your Honor."

"Still a member of the bar in good standing?"

"Yes, Your Honor."

"Taking a break from chasing the ankle-biter?" The smile widened into a grin. Judge Burdette had once been Chief State's Attorney Burdette, the (mostly) benevolent dictator of the prosecutorial service.

"Yes, ma'am. The ankle-biter is in school."

"Pictures after session, MacInnes." She took a breath and focused, briskly dismissing personal concerns. "So have you been able to reason with your recalcitrant client?"

Michael was staring. He could not have looked more stunned if Scotchie had suddenly burst into Hamlet's soliloquy.

I hoped the shock would keep him compliant.

"Yes, Your Honor," I said. "My client wishes to apologize profusely and throw himself upon the mercy of the court. In the line of an explanation– but not an excuse– he would humbly remind Your Honor that he was providing his client a zealous defense."

"Too zealous." Judge Burdette glared at Michael.

He shrank a little.

"Yes, Your Honor. Mr. Adair freely admits he went too far in the conduct of his argument. He is deeply remorseful and promises it will not happen again."

The judge looked at Michael. Held his gaze for a full thirty seconds.

Then:

"He's quite right it won't happen again. Unless he wishes to find out how many friends he has in the county lockup."

Michael gave her a nod that was almost like a bow. He did a very good chastened bad boy.

"Anything further?"

"If Your Honor would permit me," I began. "There does seem to be an evidentiary issue here, if floridly stated at considerable volume by my client."

Judge Burdette gave Michael another glare. "Very floridly."

"Indeed," I said. "But my understanding is the prosecution is asking for the admission of prior bad acts from a civil action as fact."

"Oh?" The blue laser gaze sharpened. I would not want to be the Assistant State's Attorney on the case later today.

"And considering the different standard of proof in a civil action…" I continued.

"By no means automatic, Counselor." She nodded to me. "I'll hear arguments on this Monday morning."

"Thank you, Your Honor."

She acknowledged me, then returned to scowling at Michael. "Mr. Adair, next time, start with the question of fact at a lower volume."

"Yes, Your Honor," Michael said, just loudly enough to be heard. "Very sorry, Your Honor."

"You should be." She raised a hand in a brush-off wave. "Enough. Get him out of my sight. We'll resume Monday. MacInnes, approach, with pictures."

"All rise!" Edwards called, this time a bit quieter.

Judge Burdette and I spent a good five minutes catching up and admiring kid, dog, and cat pictures. Not to push the metaphor, but the jurist is really a pussycat when she's in a kindly mood.

When she's not, well, Michael just found out.

When I rejoined him at the defense table, Michael looked from the departing judge to me and back, then stared at me for a moment. Michael let out a breath. "How did you-"

"Remember? I worked under her my first year in trial bureau."

"But still, it's Judge Burdette."

"She always liked me."

"Okay."

"And," I reminded him, "she also likes good legal reasoning. And in this case, the facts were on your side, even if your presentation of them was not."

"There's that. Thank you, Tweety."

"My pleasure."

He smiled. Wicked, wild-Scotsman smile. "We will definitely be talking about your pleasure later."

"Nice."

"Not nice at all."

I still had a bit of glow when I ransomed my car from the courthouse parking garage (rates have gone up exponentially since my prosecuting days!) and started driving back to Alcott.

I was halfway there before I remembered Michael's comment about "that SOB Winch."

I hit the speed dial. He was still at the office, probably getting a head start on the Monday evidence hearing.

"Hey, Tweety. Shiraz or cab?"

"California cab," I replied, smiling at his relaxed tone, and who are we kidding, the thought of a good bottle of wine after this day. "What SOB Winch were you talking about?"

"Morton. Husband of the dead councilwoman."

Ah-ha. And not the 80's pop band. "Thanks."

"Why?"

"I may know something. Tell you later."

"Um...okay."

"Meet me at the social."

"Yeah– get us a table, and I'll get the ice cream."

"Will do."

That SOB Winch.

CHAPTER 29
ICE CREAM ANTI-SOCIAL

I took a mental break for the rest of the drive home to Alcott, blasting the radio and just not thinking for a little while. A real treat on any day since I'm rarely in the car for long without Daniel in the back complaining about my choice of music.

Today, twenty minutes with bad power ballads was exactly what I needed, considering the exhausting evening to come.

(Yes, I actually like Celine Dion, and I sing along when I'm alone in the car. Fight me.)

I knew Corinna and I would spend two very intense hours dishing vanilla, chocolate, and strawberry, opening big squeeze bottles of syrup, and trying to keep the fifth and sixth-grade boys from weaponizing the giant cans of whipped cream. If I hadn't promised Corinna and Brian I'd back them up, I would have scooped up Daniel at the hardware store and headed home to dive into a bottle of wine.

But duty called.

Two whirlwind hours on the home front before the social even started. Somehow, I got Daniel home and into a plate of chicken nuggets, Scotchie out into the yard, switched my court suit for a sweater and skinny pants, and even put in a load of laundry after Daniel splatted ketchup on his polo.

Oh, and grabbed the scarf from the bottom of the closet and the poison container out of my jacket pocket and buried them deep in the outdoor trash can. They could go safely to the land-fill, and no one would ever have to think about them again. One more problem solved.

Michael arrived just as Daniel and I were leaving and favored us with kisses and pats on the head. If I noticed he was clearly going to get most of an hour to himself before joining us at the social, I did my best not to envy him.

He'd had a long enough day, after all.

And Scotchie would demand a walk.

At Rowland Elementary, the party was already getting started.

The event was in the multipurpose room, set up with two big serving tables in the front, and the kitchen, with the extra ice cream just a quick step behind a door at our backs. If the early crowd was any indication, we were going to need every one of those ten-gallon tubs.

The PTA's ice cream social is the school's big fall fundraiser, and a must-do for anyone who considers themselves important in town. So it was no surprise to see Ginny Pescatore sweep in soon after we got the tables set up, and start holding court– or courting voters.

Moira had set up shop at one of the front tables, with all of her Friends of the Library merch. We exchanged a wave and a careful smile on my way in, and that was all. It would take a little time for us to get back to normal, but I had no doubt we would.

As Corinna and I set up one of the sundae counters, and Brian settled into his spot at the cash box, I kept an eye on Ginny. As much as I wanted to believe I'd stumbled on something from Michael's comment about Winch, she was still a decent possi-bility for the killer. She had all the same opportunities Morton Winch had, if with different motives.

Less compelling motives, I thought, but the hungry– and not

for ice cream– look on her face as she worked the room made me wonder about that, just a little.

Also still making me wonder a bit, George Germain, who stopped at Ginny's table and had some kind of hissy whispered conversation with her. I remembered our weird little chat in the grocery store, and that Moira had placed him at the library when the poison was out, too.

I wasn't sure he was crazy enough to do it. But I could not say he wasn't crazy enough, either.

Kryssie clattered through a few minutes before the formal start of the event, adjusting the tubs of ice cream, bottles of syrup and plastic containers of sprinkles by a millimeter here and a millimeter there while fluttering her freshly-manicured hands and burbling about how exciting it all was.

I took the opportunity to pull her aside. "You've got the Book, right?"

"In my trunk, Grace. I don't have time for this now."

"That's fine. We can slip off a bit later. Just wanted to remind you."

She let out an exasperated little snort. "Fine. Now let me get this thing going."

Kryssie swanned out toward the school hallway like the leading lady greeting the fans.

Let her. As long as I left with the Book, I didn't care how we got there.

Daniel, Cherise, and Zoey took up residence at a table near the sundae setup, close enough to be within supervising range, but far enough the boring parental units weren't all up in their business. They probably had the best deal of the night: first through the sundae line, and able to sneak over for extra whipped cream and sprinkles whenever we let them.

Fair enough, considering their parents were working the event, after all.

Working it with half a brain on the ice cream, and half on assessing the suspect pool, at least in my case. Everyone who'd been at the library when Moira stepped away from the poison was there, except for Al.

Friday was his night for Sabbath dinner with his daughters, and Madge sometimes joined him, but not always. Tonight, Madge was waiting at home for word I had the Book.

I was absolutely sure Al had nothing to do with the poisoning, and I was honestly glad he was busy somewhere else while Madge and I took care of business. Maybe she'd be ready to think about that ring once the Book was in ashes.

While Al was safely out of the picture, I got a chance for a good look at the remaining contenders on the suspect list as we dished and poured, sprinkled, and sprayed. Ginny in her corner, George Germain circulating…and then Morton Winch walked in, with his zoning officer friend on his arm.

Of course he did.

Ginny was having people sign address cards at her little spot, in clear violation of PTA policy (no electioneering at school events!) and talking animatedly at an appreciative audience of mommies and a few dads. She was "on," in ways I hadn't seen before, and once again, I had to ask myself how far she would go to get what she wanted if what seemed like an easy opportunity to clear the path just opened up in front of her? The container and the open page would quite literally have looked like a sign saying, "go remove somebody."

Not to mention George Germain and his talk of karma.

He was busily upbraiding the parents running the other sundae table because the ice cream wasn't certified rBST-free and there was corn syrup in the toppings. He was absolutely crazy enough to see a sign and act on it.

No question.

I was noodling about those possibilities as I dished up ice cream until the final clue slapped me right across the face.

A scent.

An unmistakable and oppressive scent. Aftershave that could knock you down and choke you. I knew immediately where I'd smelled it before. On the scarf with the scent of poison.

Just a thread of it at the urn at Obedellia Winch's calling hours.

And now, on Morton Winch, as I handed him a bowl of ice cream.

That SOB Winch.

Good money is always on the husband.

"Oh, Grace, thank you," he said as I handed him the bowl.

"You're welcome. Would you like some whipped cream?" I asked.

"Yes, please."

"Come over here, I think I need to open a new can."

Before he realized what I was doing, I'd grabbed his arm and pulled him through the door into the empty kitchen, holding him against the wall with the only weapon at hand: the giant spray-can of whipped cream.

Ridiculous, I'm sure, but the combination of weapon and shock did the trick.

"What– Grace– why– " he sputtered, clutching the bowl in front of him as if it were some kind of defensive weapon.

I took a breath and pulled myself into ice-cold calm. Everything around this situation might be ridiculous, but the stakes were anything but.

Whipped cream or not, PTA festivities on the other side of that door notwithstanding, I had to catch and stop this killer right now. Or else.

"I know what you did. And I know how you did it."

The direct approach is always good.

"I don't understand -"

"You killed your wife with poison you found on Moira's desk."

He drew himself up and tried to look indignant. Imposing. "I don't know what you're talking about, Grace. Did Moira tell you some crazy story? She's probably falling into dementia like her mother."

"Stop it." I aimed the can where it would do the most good. *Not* at the ice cream. "Don't talk about her like that."

Winch winced. "Really, Grace. I don't know what you're-"

"There's surveillance cam video." Of course there wasn't, but he had no way to know that. And it was a credible lie. "So let's stop screwing around here."

Winch's face turned gray. Similar to the color of his wife's as the poison finished its work. Just no red line on the eyelids...yet.

He let out a deflated sigh. "All right."

"Not all right at all."

"What do you have to do with this?" he asked.

"Bad question." I said, waving the can a little. Want to find out how much that propellant stings? "You're caught and that's all you need to know."

"Are you two in some kind of coven or-"

"Do you want to find out how well that poison really works?" I asked. A much better threat.

"Um, no." He wilted a bit.

"Then stop asking questions."

"What happens now?"

"Unfortunately, you're going to get away with murder."

"Really?" The mope actually grinned. "So what-"

"You're not going to get away with corruption though. I know you were using your position as Mrs. Winch's husband to find out what was going on with the outlet mall, and your relationship with the zoning officer to move it forward. And I strongly suspect you're getting a cut of the action from someone who's already been indicted."

Each sentence deflated Winch a bit more.

By the time I finished, he was slumped over and looking like the pathetic creep he was. Still clutching the ice cream. Gollum with a bowl of empty calories.

"What happens now?" he asked.

"Now, you do the only right thing available."

He looked puzzled and more than a little scared.

Entirely reasonable fear. The Mothers expected me to keep loss of life to a minimum, but no one would argue if I had to dispose of the actual murderer to keep everything quiet.

But I really hate killing people.

Unless they've earned it.

By my standards, Winch was moving toward the line, but he wasn't there yet. I didn't want to take him out unless I had to. And with a little help from my friends, I probably wouldn't have to.

"All right," I said. "Give me your phone."

"What?" Morton Winch asked, his small olive-pit-green eyes suddenly defiant behind his glasses. "What are you going to do?"

"I'm not." I moved the can menacingly and backed it up with a glare. "You are going to call my friend in the U.S. Attorney's Office and tell her what you were up to with the outlet mall."

"But I-"

"Or, I can just call the cops. I have the poison, and I can connect you with it. And you may not realize this, but some elements of it survive cremation. How do you feel about 20 to life?"

"What?"

"If they know what they're looking for, and I'll make sure they do, a decent crime lab can find traces of it." He bought one credible lie. No reason to believe he wouldn't swallow another.

"You wouldn't."

"Want to try me?" I doubt most people could look dangerous over a whipped cream can, but I did have the glare. I turned it on, full force.

No one had ever lived to tell whether it worked, so I hoped for the best.

Morton Winch wilted a little. I caught a whiff of flop-sweat under the horrific cologne.

"All right. You and your poisoning friends win."

"I wouldn't cast aspersions, considering," I said. "The phone."

He set the ice cream down on a kitchen counter and handed over the device.

I brought up the keypad with my thumb and punched in Marisol's mobile number. It was early enough she probably wasn't at her book club yet. "Her name is Marisol Ruiz-Miller. You're not going to tell her I sent you, or anything related to the poison."

"I'm not?"

"No. You're going to tell her it was just time to come forward."

"Why?"

"Because I'm protecting everyone involved here. Even you."

"No, I'm not asking that." Winch winced again. "I mean, why am I coming forward?"

"Tell her your conscience is troubling you." I looked at him. Marisol doesn't question the dentistry on gift horses, but ascribing a conscience to this guy was a bit much. "No, forget that. Tell her you knew it was going to come out sooner or later, and you wanted to get the best deal you could."

"That's actually kind of true."

"The best lies usually are." I handed back the phone. "Now, get to it. I have to go back to slinging ice cream."

He hit send. I could tell Marisol picked up.

Morton started in a stammer, but quickly picked up speed.

Good. One problem solved.

Now back to the syrup and sprinkles.

A few minutes later, I saw Winch slink out of the multi-purpose room, casting nervous glances my way. He would do exactly as he was told because he knew the consequences could be far worse if he didn't. He might even have figured he was safer with the Feds.

And he was right.

One last problem to resolve tonight. We'd just opened the final tubs of ice cream and set out all the remaining toppings, so everyone who stayed to the end could jump in for a little free-for-all, when I saw Kryssie coming by.

"Now," I said, patting her arm. "Let's get this done now."

"But everyone-"

"Is up to their eyeballs in sugar. It'll just take a minute."

"Oh, fine." She pulled her keys out of her pocket. "Let's go."

The parking lot was barely lit, and surprisingly quiet. Nobody was going to run out in the middle of the final feast. At least not anyone who wanted their kids to keep speaking to them.

She popped her trunk and handed me the book. I pulled a twenty out of my pocket and handed it to her.

"Thanks," I forced myself to sound grateful and polite. "I really appreciate this. The Book matters a lot to Madge."

"Why?" she asked.

"Family thing."

"Really? Is it special, or valuable?" Her eyes had the same acquisitive gleam as Thursday, but this time, I had to make sure she was shut down and shut down hard.

"No. It's a sentimental family thing. That's all."

"You went to a lot of trouble for some little family thing."

"Madge is special to me."

"Is that all? Sure sounds like there's some-"

"Please don't ask any more questions."

"Why? I'm just curious and-"

"Tell you what," I replied, allowing some steel to creep into my tone, "you don't ask about my life, and I don't ask about yours."

"What does that mean?"

"I think you know."

Kryssie glared at me. "What do *you* know?"

"I know I've seen your SUV at the firehouse at a number of

odd hours." I held her gaze. "And you and a big dark-haired guy put that SUV to good use one morning not long ago."

"Well, I was just talking to some PTA parents…"

I looked at her. "That's the best you got?"

"He was showing me-"

"Please," I said, "don't tell me what he was showing you."

"There's no need to be nasty."

"Trust me, Kryssie, you'll know when I get nasty." I gave her a tinge of the glare to remind her.

"Well." She huffed. "You've got your book back."

"I do. And it would be a very bad idea for you to discuss this with anyone."

"Don't worry."

I turned for the door.

"You're still going to write the press release for the holiday choir tea, right?"

"Of course, I am."

"Good." She closed the trunk and swept past me with a happy smile. Unpleasantness forgotten, as long as she got what she wanted.

What a piece of work.

On the other hand, I didn't have to kill her either, and that was worth a lot. At least for the moment. I put the Book in my car, double-checked to be sure it was locked, then turned for the social.

The after-party was well underway.

Brian's work at the cashbox was done, so he'd come to our table to hang out with Michael and the kids. They were laughing, and as I got closer, I realized it was about Scotchie and the blue doo.

Laughing, too, I dropped a kiss on the top of Daniel's head, getting the customary brush-off, and held up a hand to Michael.

"What's up?"

"Madge has a little bit of an emergency."

The men gave me concerned glances.

"Not a bad emergency, a good one. Al proposed, and she needs to talk it out. Do you mind getting Daniel home after the knockdown?"

"I love a good emergency for a change." Michael said. "Sure thing."

"Tell her to say yes," Brian added.

"That's exactly what I'm going to do." It wasn't a lie. I had been planning for days to tell Madge to stop fighting Al.

"Absolutely," Michael agreed. "Good standup guy."

Brian beamed. "Be nice to have a wedding to look forward to."

"Especially since we don't have to plan it." Michael gave me a naughty glance. "Can I wear my kilt?"

"I'd be disappointed if you didn't."

"So would I," Brian said, and he and Michael shared a high-five.

Corinna waved to me from the almost empty ice cream tubs. Back to work. Not fair to leave her with this mess.

"See you back at the house," I called to Michael.

"Hopefully with good news."

He had no idea how good.

CHAPTER 30
INTO THE FIRE

C orinna accepted my abject apology for abandoning her in the whirlwind, especially after I offered to take care of cleaning up our table so she could leave with the kids. Clay had worked late and apparently offered to open a nice bottle of wine, and handle bedtime, in return for missing the social.

That was a deal no woman with a brain would turn down, and I happily sent her on the way. We'd catch up later.

Kryssie, no surprise, disappeared during the final cleanup, so I ended up walking to my car with a couple of new kindergarten parents who'd stayed late because they were trying too hard. They were actually kind of cute.

When I, and the Book, were finally safe and alone in my car, I sat there in the dark for a second, a little shellshocked. It was almost over.

Almost. There was at least a very real possibility we were going to pull this off.

One of the kindergarten parents knocked on my window.

"Are you okay?" she asked.

"Fine." I waved and started the car. "Just been a really long day."

"Oh, I know that one," she said.

Somehow, I doubted it.

Now, on to the Book burning.

I hope you know by now I'm not a fan of book burnings. But this one Book had to be burned to keep everyone safe. So bring on the fire, baby.

On the drive to Madge's, I heard my phone beep. In her driveway, I read the text from Marisol:

I don't know what you did, but thank you.

Don't ask.

Don't worry, I won't.

I sent a smiley, grabbed the Book, and got out of the car.

Madge was waiting and ready. A nice big blaze was well alight in her fireplace, the glow warming her face.

When she opened the door, she smiled, the first real, relaxed smile I'd seen from her since that day in the park.

"Oh, thank God." The smile widened into a full-face grin, "Or maybe the Archangel."

"Something like that," I agreed. "All's well that ends."

Connery, from his usual spot on the hearth rug, looked up at me and yawned.

Everything's fine if the cat isn't impressed.

"I've already told the Mothers we have it. They want a picture of it in the fire."

"I don't blame them." I held out the Book and got my first really good look. "No wonder."

"No wonder what?"

I turned the front to Madge. "This is why Al thought it was one of those *Great Novels*."

Madge stared for a moment, then shook her head and sighed. At some point, Eliza MacNeish had stenciled "The Sisters" on the cover. The fancy old lettering in gold was almost exactly like the kind of thing favored by the old book subscription club.

If I hadn't recognized the usual purple binding, I might well have made the same mistake.

"Well, isn't that a pip," Madge said. "Check it, and burn it."

I opened the Book. And right in front, as expected, purple ink in a spidery shaky hand crept across the flyleaf. The recipe in all its glory, complete with detailed instructions, and that breathtakingly foolish title. If I hadn't seen it– and hadn't lived the last week– I would not have believed it. "Here. Get the flyleaf with the name– and that damn recipe."

Madge shook her head. "It's a good thing I didn't find out about this until I was cleaning out her place."

"Yeah?"

"Yeah. Something would have had to happen."

Like it almost had to happen to her. Maybe to us. I took a breath, nodded. "Well, it didn't. And thank the good Lord for that."

"Absolutely. And the Archangel." She held out her phone. "Trade you. I'll put it in the fire, you take the picture."

"Works for me."

As we moved in, Connery got up, snorted, and stalked away. No matter how important the situation, it is not important enough to disturb the cat. Just ask him.

I clicked off a couple of shots as Madge took the Book, holding it open for a moment to show the flyleaf. Then she bent down and placed it, still open, on the logs. I snapped a few more pics as it caught, and the flames began to chew up the pages.

We stood in silence, watching, for a moment.

"Well, that's done," Madge said finally.

"And well done." I took a long breath. Weirdly, the room was filled with a sweet scent, almost like incense. "Do you smell that?"

"Yes." She sniffed deeply and held my gaze. "It's said that angels sometimes announce their presence with a pleasing scent."

"Really."

"It's also said that old books often had flowers pressed

between the pages, which might release their essential oils when burned."

Could go either way.

For a few more seconds, we stood there watching the fire.

Better not to think too much about this.

On the mantel, there was a picture of Madge, her late husband, and their son. And one of Al.

"When are you going to tell him 'Yes?'" I asked, a little surprised by my own bluntness.

"Already did." Shy smile. "Figured he should know I was all-in, whatever ended up happening."

"Oh, that is wonderful!"

She held out her arms, and we hugged.

Connery yowled.

"Is he going to be okay with the other fella in your life?" I asked, nodding to the cat.

"We'll figure it out." She nodded to the fire with another relieved smile. "Since we're going to get the chance."

"We weren't going to let it end any other way," I assured her. Now that we were safe, it was okay– even wise– to believe we'd been certain to find a resolution. "And now we get to plan a wedding."

"Well, yes. But first, you get to go home to that wonderful Scotsman of yours."

"Throwing me out because your man's coming over?"

"You caught me." A really adorable blush. "Shabbat dinner is over, and he wants some couple time."

"Good thing."

"The best. Happy Feast of the Archangels." She held out a card and a small box of candy.

"Oh, no." I shook my head. "Your card– and some of those nice Swiss truffles– are sitting in my desk at home."

"I always say you shouldn't have, Grace, but this year, I'm not kidding. Keep the truffles after all this."

We shared a laugh.

"You'll still get the card, though," I assured her.

One more laugh and happy hug, and I took off for my own, actually pretty great, life. I was in the car, driving the few blocks home when the hands-free lit up. A new and different unfamiliar number. It could have been a spammer, but I was pretty sure it wasn't.

"Hello?"

"Well done, Grace."

Unmistakable voice. I hadn't been her student for nearly twenty years, but Professor Munroe's praise still warmed me.

"Thank you, Professor."

"I assume the other matter has been handled, as well."

"In a very satisfactory and bloodless fashion."

"Bloodless?"

"Yes. No one person knew enough of the details to be a threat. And the actual killer is being punished for another crime, so some form of justice is being done."

"Justice is a very good thing."

"I think so too. You'll know all the details later, but he's likely to end up in prison for a corruption scheme and bring down several others with him."

"Excellent. There's no need to leave bodies across the landscape." Her tone was back to the usual warm and wonderful. "Unless we're being paid for it, of course."

"Of course."

"At any rate, Grace, I'm quite proud of you."

"I'm really glad to hear that." She had no idea how glad.

"Happy Feast of the Archangels a bit early, Grace. The Mothers are well pleased."

"Happy Feast of the Archangels to you, Professor. Hope you enjoy the roses."

"I absolutely will now." She sounded as relieved as I felt. "I should probably send you some, as well."

"Please don't. Michael would notice that."

"Ah, the Scotsman. No, we can't trouble him. So just accept my compliments and know you've done good work."

"More than enough, Professor."

More indeed.

CHAPTER 31
THE (FUDGE) FEAST OF
THE ARCHANGELS

A nd so, the conquering heroine heads for home.

Well, that's a bit excessive, but I sure felt pretty darn victorious. The Book safely destroyed, secrets kept, friends protected...and Obedellia Winch's murderer facing at least some kind of punishment. Even if it probably would end up as a relatively short time-out in Club Fed.

After a mess like this, you take your win where you get it.

Scotchie met me at the door, pinning me to the wall as usual, for a thorough sniff and face-lick. He seemed more interested than usual in my scent, and I wondered for a moment if he picked up something from the burning Book. But come on, it's a dog.

Once I was properly greeted, Scotchie followed me to Daniel's room to help Michael and I tuck him in, happily draping himself over the foot of the bed to watch his boy.

Michael gave Daniel a kiss and left, but I stayed for a while to watch him doze off in a sugar overload haze. There's still a lot of baby in his round face, especially when he sleeps, and he still snuggles up to me like he did when he was tiny.

I spent longer than usual watching Daniel and treasuring the moment. Before I knew it, he would be a spiky teen like Corinna's Imani. I hoped he'd still love and need me. At least a little.

Worry about that when I get there, I supposed.

After this ugly donnybrook, it felt like a luxury to contemplate something in the far future. A luxury to realize I was going to have one.

Once Daniel was asleep, I went into the kitchen, where that good California cab was breathing, just waiting for us. If Michael and I hadn't earned a good glass of wine tonight…

Earned it more than he ever needed to know.

I took the clip out of my hair, poured two glasses, and headed into the living room.

Michael was on the couch, jacket off, tie loose, looking at his phone, his expression a little dazed.

"Morton Winch turned himself in for the Alcott outlet mall development scheme. Just got word from your old pal Marisol at the U.S. Attorney."

"Really."

"Really. She thanks you for getting her out of book club. She and her wife are taking us to dinner sometime soon."

"Great idea."

"Definitely." Michael gave me a sharp assessing look for a moment, before taking a breath and shrugging. "That makes life a lot easier. With Winch and the outlet mall in the mix, I should be able to negotiate a pretty decent deal for my client. I may not even need to fight with Judge Burdette."

"Not a bad ending."

I handed Michael his glass.

"Not bad at all." He patted the cushion beside him. "Sit down and relax for a while, Tweety."

I sat.

We clinked and drank, our eyes holding as we did.

This was the time it was hardest not to tell him, when we were close, when he looked at me with that bottomless love and respect. Like he would trust and cherish me no matter what.

And I knew, a dozen years in, that he would. As I would him.

The motto of the Scottish Clan Adair is *Loyal Unto Death* for a reason.

"C'mere." Michael put his glass down and leaned back on the couch, reaching for me.

"Don't have to ask me twice." I put mine down, and let him pull me in, enjoying the warmth as he wrapped his arms around me. I rested my head on his shoulder, and he buried his face in my hair.

For a few breaths, we stayed twined together, no reason to say anything. Wonderful.

"Do I need to know why Morton Winch suddenly decided to come forward?" he asked finally.

"Nope."

"So there's no particular reason he decided to turn himself in to your old classmate in the U.S. Attorney's Office?"

"Um…"

"After a little encouragement at the ice cream social, say?"

I snuggled in a little closer. "Let's just say I hear things, and I was able to administer a bit of encouragement based on that."

"Fair enough. There's nothing I'm going to need to know about?"

It is a very good thing to be married to a man who understands sometimes it is more dangerous to know than to not know. Especially if he happens to be the defense attorney you call when you're *really* in trouble in New Haven County. Even better that I wasn't going to need him. Professionally.

"Not even a little," I assured him.

"Good." His arms tightened around me. "I don't say it enough, Tweety-Bird," he said, his tone the soft low one he reserved for me. "I love you."

"I love you."

The knot that had been in my stomach since I saw the red line on Mrs. Winch's eyelids was finally relaxing. It was really over. We were safe. All of us.

"If you were into something dangerous, you'd tell me."

"I would." ...never unless I had absolutely no other option.

"And I'd help you. Whatever it was. You're my wife, and the mother of our son, and I'll protect you."

"I know." I slipped my hand into one of his and laced fingers. It was far more likely I would end up protecting him, but I was more than happy to stay in his happy cocoon of assumptions for the moment.

"Just needed to say it." Michael kissed the top of my head. "Sorry to be a Neanderthal."

"The Neanderthals were actually a very advanced civilization...and possibly even matriarchal."

"Matriarchal is good. I know who's the real steel here."

"Yeah?"

"I was pretty impressed today." He pulled back enough to look in my eyes. "Maybe you should be doing less copy editing and more arguing."

"Ya think?"

"I don't suppose you'd be willing to second-chair once in a while..."

"*Second*-chair?"

Michael gave me a sheepish little smile. "Maybe guest-star?"

"I'm teasing. I like it."

"Yeah?" His smile widened. "Good. I liked seeing you argue instead of staring at a screen for a change."

"I liked it too."

"Not that you're not good at the other stuff..."

"It's okay. I know you respect my work."

"You're pretty amazing." His admiring gaze was pretty amazing. "I've never seen *anyone* handle Judge Burdette like that. And you got me the hearing, too."

"I have special skills."

I was joking, but his expression was serious.

"You sure do." Admiration, and something else, in his tone. "I'm just glad you're on my side...and the side of the angels."

If there is anything on earth hotter than a good-looking man who respects you as a professional, I don't know what it is. It was how Michael won me in the first place, and it never fails.

And he knows it.

I picked up my glass and nodded to his. "Adair and Adair then."

He took his glass with a grin. We clinked and drank.

"Now, about those special skills," he said, a familiar hot glow kindling in his green-gold eyes. "We can finish the wine later."

It was only much later, after I'd enjoyed Michael's *other* special skills, slipped into the kitchen, and made a new batch of fudge, that I caught something else.

As I surrendered to the sugar hit of that first wonderful bite, the smooth chocolate melting on my tongue, I remembered the note in Michael's voice, the gleam in his eyes...and that comment about being on the side of the angels.

Only then did I wonder if he was referring to more than my expertise with precedent.

I took another bite of rich silky fudge. Since it was now officially the Feast of the Archangels, and everything was safely settled, I might as well have another piece.

As for Michael and me, we could burn that bridge when we came to it.

DEATH BY CHOCOLATE FUDGE

(BASED ON ORIGINAL HERSHEY'S COCOA RECIPE)

3 cups sugar

2/3 cup cocoa

1/8 teaspoon salt

1 ½ cups milk

¼ cup butter (half stick)

1 teaspoon vanilla

½ cup chopped nuts (my grandmother would throw them at
you, but go ahead if you're into that!)

Line eight-inch-square pan with buttered paper. Mix sugar, cocoa, and salt in a heavy saucepan, then stir in milk. Cook over medium heat, stirring constantly until the mixture reaches a full rolling boil. Then cook without stirring until sugar reaches soft ball stage (236-238 degrees Fahrenheit). Remove from heat. Add butter and vanilla without stirring. Once mixture is lukewarm (110 degrees) beat with wooden spoon until candy is thick and loses its gloss. Stir in nuts – if you must – and turn out into a lightly-buttered eight-inch square pan. Mark in pieces while warm, cut when cold and firm.

Makes enough for one hit mom and her clueless family.

DEATH BY CHOCOLATE FUDGE
(BASED ON ORIGINAL HERSHEY'S COCOA RECIPE)